CAUGHT DEAD TO WRITE

A CAT LATIMER MYSTER

LYNN CAHOON

CAUGHT DEAD TO WRITE – A Cat Latimer Mystery.
Lynn Cahoon

THE CAT LATIMER MYSTERIES
A STORY TO KILL

Fatality by Firelight
Of Murder and Men
Slay in Character
Sconed to Death
A Field Guide to Homicide
A Killer Christmas Wish
Caught Dead to Write

Novellas:
Body in the Book Drop

Acknowledgement
Big thanks to Megan Kelly of MKBooksEditing for her close eye and
insightful questioning.

1

———

Cat Latimer's mom always said the kitchen is the heart of the home. The saying was true in the Aspen Hill, Colorado house where Cat grew up and equally as true in the Warm Spring's house across town where she now lived. However, this kitchen wasn't Cat's domain. Instead, it belonged to Shauna Marie Clodagh, Cat's best friend and partner in the Warm Springs Writers' Retreat. They hosted the retreat on-site every month. It wasn't unusual to find Cat and Shauna huddled around the kitchen table discussing the upcoming retreat like they were this evening or planning for future sessions. Most days, their meetings didn't involve much more than enjoying a cup of coffee together.

This month they needed to rethink their plan again. The writers were arriving on Saturday, two days early. Cat and Shauna, along with the local bookstore owner, Tammy Jones, sponsored a costume party for the retreat guests, as well as locals who attended the bookstore's writing group. Cat had invited some of the Covington College English Department staff as well since Covington sponsored the writing retreat. But now, she wondered why she'd made that offer of goodwill since they were trying to bite her hand off.

She pointed to the letter on the table. "Seriously, they want to cancel our contract because the writers who attend the sessions aren't literary enough. They must realize that genre authors kick butt as far as making money is concerned. Don't they want to be on the good side of people who might be inclined to sponsor a scholarship someday?"

"Cat, it's *one* professor who's upset, not the entire department. I bet the Dean's only holding this hearing to discuss both sides. When you bring in our stats showing how successful our retreat graduates have been, they'll see our side." Shauna got up and stirred the pot of chili on the stove. Her red hair was pulled into a clip, and with the apron she always wore, Shauna looked like she'd stepped out of time or from an Old West movie. The oven alarm went off and she pulled out a pan of spicy corn bread, filling the kitchen with the warm fresh baked smell. "Seth complained the other day that he hasn't had time to make his chili this fall. So, I made it for him. I hope I got the ingredients right. He's more of a by feel chef than a follow the recipe kind."

"Cook, not chef," Cat corrected her. "Seth just likes to putter and he really only knows one dish, his chili. He'll love it. How has he been? I haven't seen him around. Lately, I've just focused on this deadline and the retreat, I guess."

"You're hiding in your office. You're both about as stubborn as an elderly mule. He misses you when you don't stop by. I don't know why you don't just move into the other wing with him. I know the wedding got put off after his deployment, but..."

"Canceled, not delayed. And I don't want to talk about it." Cat held up her hand to stop the conversation. "Besides, it's not my decision. Seth is the one who decided to not get married."

"Because he didn't know if he was coming back. And he did. You have to realize you have a lot of people in your life who care about you." Shauna cut the corn bread and dished up two bowls of chili. "Can you take Seth's dinner over to him tonight? You can carve out an hour of your day for him. The book will wait. And you two need to talk."

Cat held up the letter. "And what about this?"

"The only thing we can do is attend the hearing and tell our side.

If Covington wants to cancel our contract, we'll find the money. Having a paying guest in place of their student will make up some of that deficit. Once Seth finishes remodeling the other wing, we'll have more rooms open for guests sooner than later. Or we could add a second session each month. Or maybe several months out of the year." Shauna held out the tray with their dinner on it. "Just don't worry about it now. We have a lot of options. And time. The only thing you need to think about is your deadline, the retreat, and Seth. The rest of the stuff is just details."

"When did you get to be the Zen one? But you're right. Nothing I can do about their decision after the hearing." Cat took the tray Shauna handed her, then set it on the table. She added a plate with several of Shauna's fresh baked cookies for the retreat. "I'll have dinner with Seth. Sit and talk for a while unless he's in a mood. Then I'll be back in my office writing if you need me. What time is Seth going to Denver to pick up the guests tomorrow?"

"Noon. He should be back by four. And the party starts at six. They're coming in from California this time around. They're in a writing group sponsored by that bookstore you loved visiting so much. You need to get it on your travel schedule again when you release next year." Shauna put a glass of milk and a sparkling water on the tray.

"South Cove? I loved that bookstore. The owner was really nice, but the event planner, she was a hoot." Cat picked up the tray. "And these are paranormal authors?"

"Actually, I think their link is this bookstore. The fact we're having a costume party was just a bonus for them." Shauna grabbed a bowl from the cupboard. "I'm going to make another batch of cookies for the party before I eat dinner. I'll see you in the morning?"

"You'll probably see me when I bring the tray back."

Shauna opened the fridge and started pulling out ingredients. "Unless I'm out feeding Snow and the dwarfs. I swear I've never seen a horse be as friendly with a bunch of cats in my life. They're all buddies."

"Snow's a good parental figure." Cat left the kitchen, pushing the door open with her back. "Thanks for pulling me off the ledge. I can't believe this Professor Barring got under my skin again. I promise I'll put it away until after the retreat. Then I'll go slash her tires."

"Sure, you will." Shauna laughed as she waved Cat out of the kitchen. "Go feed your man. He's probably starving."

"He's not my man anymore. He's just a friend. And if I can't slash her tires, then I'll turn mice loose in her lecture hall." Cat mused as she walked away. What else could she do to an English professor whose snobby attitude failed to see the joy and creativity that commercial fiction brought the world? "I guess I'm just going to have to find a way to convince her."

A meow from Angelica let her know she wasn't alone in the hallway. The momma cat had come to live with Cat and Shauna about the same time as Snow had arrived at the barn. Cat had rescued the feline from a local Old West tourist site that had closed down for the season. Angelica had brought a surprise with her. Four kittens. Now they had a little family in the barn, but Angelica liked being inside more than her offspring.

"Hey, sweet girl. Do you want to go visit Seth with me? You know Sam's going to want to play." Cat opened the door that led to the other wing, but at the mention of Seth's dog, Angelica turned and went the other way. Probably to sun herself in the dining room. "Okay then, I'll tell him you said hi."

She closed the door with her foot and followed the hall until it opened up into a small living room. Seth had set up his office in the room along with his gaming television and a bookcase of DVDs. He'd moved his stuff out of the apartment when he'd left that spring and into this empty room. Now, a month after he'd returned, he'd made it a home. She set the tray on a side table and turned down the volume on the television. A movie was playing, one that Cat knew Seth had watched a thousand times. But that and a fire in the fireplace was the only sign of life. "Seth? Where are you? Dinner is served."

Sam came running out of the hallway that led to the small kitchen. He had his own door to the backyard from that room. Seth and Uncle Pete had fenced a section of the yard around the door to allow Sam some yard space. Since she'd been the one to babysit Sam during Seth's absence, the dog had bonded to her as well. There was a nice swing and a small grill for summer nights on a deck. Seth liked sitting outside and she found him there a lot.

"Hey, buddy, where's your guy?" She reached down and gave Sam's head a rub. He greeted her, then went to sniff the table and the tray of food. "Nope, that's not yours but if you need something, I'll feed you."

Seth chuckled from the hallway where he stood, leaning on the doorway. He'd returned from his last deployment with a limp he wouldn't talk about and a cane. "Don't let him fool you. I fed him at three, so now he's just begging. How's the book going?"

She wanted to cross the room and give him a kiss, or at least, brush the hair out of his eyes. He needed a haircut. But their relationship had been strained since he'd announced his plans to join up with his old crew and deploy one more time. He'd worked for a private contractor and that was all he'd told her. Now he'd come home, a little banged up and a lot less cheerful. She put on a smile she didn't feel and answered his question. "Great. If I get at least a few words a day during the retreat, I still have a hope of finishing by the deadline. Remind me again why I decided hosting monthly retreats were a good idea? It's always messing with my writing schedule."

"You love your writer friends coming and playing with you. And you know it. I've decided I'm going to be Frankenstein in progress for the party tomorrow night. That way I don't look out of place with my slower pace." He waved his cane, then moved toward his chair. "Shauna made me chili? She's a peach."

"She said she hoped it met with your high standards." Cat cleared off an end table to set the tray between the two chairs. "When do you go back to the doctor? Are you sure you're up to doing the airport run tomorrow?"

"Week after next. Don't worry, it's on Shauna's calendar too so she's planning on going with me just in case, if you're still writing this book." He picked up a piece of corn bread and slathered butter on it. "I appreciate you both helping out, but I'm feeling like a bother. I think if you look up loser in the dictionary, they have a picture of me."

"You didn't mean to get hurt." Cat wanted to say so much more, but she didn't want this meal to end up in a fight. Like so many other dinners had before he left. "Besides, you're not a bother. No matter what happens between you and me, we're still friends. And you're still my contractor for the retreat."

"I'm not sure how I feel about you being so relaxed about our relationship status. But anyway, Sam and I appreciate you being so understanding. Otherwise, we'd be homeless and starving." He took a bite of the chili. "So good. I think it's better than what I make."

"I'll tell Shauna. She'll be pleased. Anyway, you wouldn't be homeless. Remember, we had the money talk before when we were going to get married. I know you have savings. I just like to keep my contractor nearby while we're in the middle of a remodel."

"I think you're trying too hard to be low key about you and me. Cat, we need to talk about the wedding." He set the bowl down. "About us. You need to know why I took that job."

"I don't know why." The words came out sharp. She took a breath, closing her eyes to keep the tears away. She didn't want him to say that he didn't love her anymore. Because then, she'd have to accept it was over. "Give me this week. I promise, after the retreat and after the book is done, we'll sit down and have that conversation. I just can't now."

He didn't speak for a long time. Then he buttered another piece of corn bread, not meeting her gaze. "Did Shauna update you on the guests for this week?"

"They're all from a little coastal tourist town in California. One of the writers backed out last month and we didn't have time to replace them, but we have four guests plus the Covington student, so that should work. Anyway, a few years ago, I did a book signing at this little store in South Cove. The bookstore there has a writers group like Tammy does, so when we found out they were coming, Shauna decided to put on this party to get the groups together."

Cat mixed in some crackers with the chili as it was just a little spicier than she liked. "Our Covington student writes poetry. So that should be fun. Not. From what Shauna said, we've got a paranormal romance writer, a woman's fiction with paranormal elements writer, and a guy who works at the bookstore and writes some sort of time travel. I'm not sure we'll offer any value to a poetry student. But I'm going to set up a session on word choices in a manuscript which should give him something out of the retreat besides time to write and time with other writers."

"You always say that the way the group clicks is the magic behind the retreats. It doesn't matter what anyone writes, you all need that networking to remind yourself you're not alone and your work has value." He stopped when he noticed Cat staring at him. "What, did I say something wrong?"

She shook her head. "No, I'm just always amazed at how someone with no writing experience can understand me so thoroughly. You're amazing, Seth Howard."

He held a finger up to correct her. "Actually, you're wrong. Not about the amazing part. That you were totally on point with. I do have writing experience. Remember I made that hiking field guide that we used with the outdoor writers that one retreat? I've still got a ton of those so next summer, I'll be back to adding value to your retreat schedule."

"You always add value, Seth." She leaned back in her chair and ate more chili. Sam curled up on the floor between them, waiting for someone to drop a piece of cornbread that needed cleaned up. Even with the elephant in the room, having dinner together tonight felt right. She thought that this might have been a glimpse into what their future would have held had they gotten married in June. A future that didn't look like it going to happen. But she needed to put this away until after the retreat. And the book. And the hearing.

She took a deep breath to calm herself.

Shauna was right. Even if the college removed their sponsorship from the retreat, they'd be fine. Life was always challenging, but there was always a new path to take when the current path presented a roadblock. She just had to find it.

2

Tammy Jones and Andi Grammy were outside stacking boxes on the porch at six the next morning. Tammy owned the local bookstore and Andi was a retreat alumni. Cat was on the stairs, coming down for more coffee when she saw them out the window. She hurried over to open the door. "What are you doing out so early?"

Tammy walked in and put the box she'd been carrying on the floor in the hallway. "We've come to help Shauna decorate. Didn't she tell you?"

"I've been trying to keep the party planning details off Cat's plate since she's on deadline." Shauna appeared out of the kitchen. "You should have called when you got here. I could have helped unpack the van."

"Andi offered to help bring things over and decorate so I can go back and open the store at ten." Tammy waved the other woman inside. "She's basically taken over the writers group for me this year. I don't know what I'd do without her."

"I'm not doing all that much. Besides, it's fun." Andi smiled at Cat and Shauna. "It's good to see you both. I talked to Mom last night and told her I was helping with the party. She said to apologize again for her behavior. She's living in Florida now helping out my grandmother. And she's taking scuba lessons. Can you believe it?"

"Well, that's amazing." Cat thought about the woman she'd met a few years ago and marveled at the changes. "And how are you?"

"This is my last year at Covington. I'm working with the career center and I think there are several paths I could take. But I'm looking at doing some sort of job around editing. I'd like to really get to know the publishing industry, you know?" She set the box she'd been carrying down by the one Tammy had brought inside. "But if we're hosting a party tonight, we better get moving."

Cat liked the new, assertive Andi. She'd been one of the students that Covington had sent to the retreat, and it had been a turning point in her life. For more reasons than one. "Then I'm off for more coffee and more words. Have fun decorating."

"Write hard," Andi called after her.

When Cat came down for a snack, the foyer was empty. The party magic was complete. Shauna and her helpers had transformed the public space into party central. Tables with books and candles circled the hallway. Fairy lights hung all the way around the walls and up the stairs. When the party started and they turned down the lights, the area was going to sparkle. Cat went into the kitchen.

Shauna mixed something by the stove and looked up when Cat came in. "It's pretty, right? Andi has a good eye for decorating."

"It's nice." Cat took her empty coffee carafe to the sink and went to the fridge for a bottle of water. "I'm hungry but I don't want a big meal. I'm going to write until the guests get here, then I'll play hostess for a bit before changing into my costume."

"I'm warming up some soup and making more cornbread for lunch. But dinner's all about the party. So make sure you eat while you're chatting. And there will be more than just cookies available." Shauna looked up from her mixing. "Do you want something now?

Seth's eating before he goes to Denver so he'll be here probably in about thirty minutes if you want to join him."

"I'll take a bowl of cereal now up to my office." Cat sidestepped the offer. "I'll eat later, just before the writers get here. That way, I'm not starving at the party and making a fool of myself."

"I'd say that was a well-thought-out plan if I didn't know it was a total dodge to keep from seeing Seth. What happened last night when you talked?" Shauna set the mixer down and walked over to where Cat was pouring milk into her cereal. "Don't tell me you got into a fight again."

"No fight. It was fine. We ate and talked about the retreat." Cat put the milk away. With her back turned from Shauna, she added, "He wants to talk about us. But I put it off until after the book gets turned in and the hearing. He said he understood. I guess telling me he doesn't love me anymore might get a little easier if I have time to prepare myself before he lowers the bad news."

"Don't think that way. Seth loves you. Even my jaded heart can see that." Shauna came up behind Cat and squeezed her shoulders. "Have faith."

Cat headed upstairs with her cereal and a fresh carafe of coffee. The best thing about being a writer was she could get lost in the story and forget about all the stuff going on in the real world. It would all be there when she came back downstairs, but for a few hours, she could make the world the way she wanted.

By the time she'd finished writing and editing for the day, Seth had left for Denver. She found Shauna sitting in the kitchen with Uncle Pete. Cat filled a bowl with soup and took it to the table to join them.

"Hey, Cat. I wondered if you'd come out of your cave to see your uncle today or not." Pete Edwards was her mom's brother, and since her parents moved to Florida, the only family she had in Aspen Hills. The fact he was the town's police chief was a bonus in Cat's eyes. Especially when she needed help with a retreat issue. Like the time she'd found a guest dead in his bedroom. Okay, so twice she'd needed help with that type of problem.

Cat pushed the memory aside and took a piece of corn bread, slathering butter over it. "I would be down here to greet you if you'd announce you were coming. You can't just pop in and expect me to know you're here. I'm not a mind reader."

"No? I would have thought you'd figure out I show up for lunch or dinner just before you start one of these retreats. I brought the background check results with me, and Shauna was nice enough to offer to feed me." He tapped a folder that sat on the table next to him.

"Anything I should know about?" Uncle Pete had talked Cat into this step after one of the retreat guests turned out to be a stalker. She still thought it was overkill, but it made him more comfortable.

"No. One person's got some parking tickets. Another was arrested at a demonstration against a business who apparently doesn't believe in global warming. And that's about it. I would have thought with the group being from California, you might have a few drug-related issues, but they look clean." His gaze dropped to the file like he considered digging deeper.

"You're profiling an entire state now? Maybe you should expect clean reports like I do since, as writers, we're a little boring. We like to watch the world experience things, not do them ourselves. Especially the arrest thing. I'm not sure I could deal with a night or more in a cell." She sipped her soup. Potato chowder. One of her favorites.

"You're a little naïve, my dear." Uncle Pete went on to tell her all about several issues bed and breakfast owners were having in Denver.

She met Shauna's gaze. "But, Uncle Pete, those places are in Denver, not Aspen Hills. Besides, they don't cater to writers. And finally, they don't have you popping in all the time. Speaking of, are you coming to the party tonight?"

"I'm not much for dressing up in costume." He leaned back and studied the two women at the table. "I guess having Seth here full time now eases my concern a bit about the two of you living with four strangers for a week."

"Five," Shauna corrected. When she saw Pete's frown, she added. "The Covington student is just as much a stranger as the writers.

And, with Covington's family clientele, I'm thinking we're safer with the random writers. Besides, you've already done the background checks, and nothing popped out. You really should come to the party though."

"Sorry, Shirley and I have our virtual date tonight. If I cancelled, she'd be on a plane from Alaska to check out who I was attending said party with. The woman keeps a tight leash on me, even from Anchorage." He finished his soup and wrapped a piece of cornbread in a napkin. "I've got to get back to the house. My cleaner's there and she'll be waiting for me to write her a check."

"Maybe we should hire her to help out with retreat week." Cat took a bite of cornbread then noticed Shauna staring at her. "What? What did I say?"

"Don't you think I keep the house clean enough?" Shauna asked, clearly offended.

Cat held up a hand. "Don't get upset. I'm saying that we should look into hiring a cleaner as a time saver for you. You cook, clean, and manage the retreat. And that's on top of writing your cookbooks. Not to mention the horse and cats and the barn."

"Seth's handling the landscaping, the construction, and keeping the barn clean and stocked. All I do is feed Snow and ride her. I'm feeling like a slacker."

Cat laughed as she swept her arm around the kitchen, showing off the plates of cookies on every flat surface. "If there's one word that doesn't describe you it's slacker. You're the most driven and productive person I know. Just look at the baking you did for the party you arranged, at the retreat you set up. I'm not sure you can fit anything else into your days without you giving something up like cleaning. You have other things you should be doing."

"My cut is based on the chores I do for the retreat. I don't want you to cut my pay either. Although technically, I really don't need the money, but my investment guy is always trying to get me to stash some away for retirement. You know that day's going to sneak up on us."

"You two are too young to be thinking about retirement," Pete said. "Now me, I'm going to have to work until I'm ninety the way the town pension keeps changing. Shirley's trying to get me to open some sort of account where it doesn't count against your taxes. Maybe I can have her come over the next time she's in town and she can explain it to all of us. I'm just don't understand what she's saying half the time. That woman is crazy smart."

"Sure, that would be fun," Cat said, meeting Shauna's gaze with a wide eyed look.

Uncle Pete stood and took his bowl to the sink. "Thanks for lunch. Have fun at your party tonight, but don't do anything that needs police attention. I'm on call tonight and I didn't tell Shirley. She gets put out if our date nights are interrupted."

Cat said her goodbyes to her uncle and then focused on Shauna. "You're so much more than just what you do for the retreat. You've got to know that."

"On the outside, probably. But I still want to pull my share here." She looked around the cozy kitchen. "I can't believe how soon I've gotten used to this place. It's home."

"It is. And you need to remember that. No matter what happens with the retreat, this is still your home. Unless you and your secret admirer run off together. Then I'll have to teach Seth to cook."

Shauna stood and took her bowl to the sink, then she cleaned off the counter. "What makes you think I have a secret admirer?"

"Flowers have come every Monday for a couple of months. And some nights when you come home, your cheeks are red, and it's not just from you walking home in the cold."

"You need to stop investigating my life. You just keep those skills to drive your uncle crazy on his unsolved cases."

Cat sighed. "You have a point. But someday, you're going to tell me, right?"

Shauna held up her hand and made a gesture. "Scout's honor."

"I don't think you were ever a scout." Cat leaned back into her chair. "I guess I'll go up and try to write some more. Sometimes getting words is like squeezing a rock and expecting lemon juice."

"Maybe having writers here will help you log in more words. You tend to get a little competitive when you all do writing sprints." Shauna moved the empty plate where the cornbread had been and wiped the table. "At least, that's what I heard."

"I'm not competitive. I just like setting a good example. It's not my fault that I can really type fast at times." Cat put her bowl in the sink. "I should have asked. Do you need help with anything before I go back to my office?"

Shauna gently pushed her toward the door. "I'm fine. Go work. You know you want to."

Cat grabbed a soda out of the fridge. "Actually, I don't. I hate it when I get this way just before a deadline. I want the book to be done, yes, but I really don't want to work. I think I'm afraid I won't be able to pull off the magic this time."

"You're always able to finish. Don't doubt yourself. I know we've had a lot on our plates. Maybe after this retreat, you and Seth should take a vacation together. Figure out what you need from him to forgive and talk this out." Shauna used her ice cream scoop to drop cookie dough on the baking sheet.

"Better idea. Let's go on a double date. You and secret admirer and me and Seth."

Shauna snorted but didn't meet Cat's gaze. "I'm not that stupid."

"So, you think it would be a bad idea? You don't think they'd like us?" Cat pushed but Shauna held up a hand.

"I'm done talking. Stop stalling and go write."

Cat left the kitchen and headed up the three flights of stairs to her office. The one good thing about having her turret office was it kept guests out of her hair during retreats. And she didn't need a stair machine.

Shauna was being really secretive about the guy she was dating. Which made Cat want to know even more who it was.

She pushed the question off and focused on her main character, Tori, and her new college. She'd joined a sorority that was keeping her busy, as well as the campus coven, who mostly hated the sorority girls. It was a balancing act for Tori to keep the two groups separate. Especially since campus wasn't that big. And of course, there were two guys. The nerdy human who read her poetry and took her on surprise picnic lunches. And the warlock who had a Harley and enjoyed long rides in the country. She was sure neither one was Tori's soul mate, but college was time to have some fun. And it was Cat's job to make the fun screw up her life as much as possible.

She opened her pop and sat at her desk, reading the last paragraph she'd written before lunch. Then she set her watch alarm for an hour and started writing. Shauna was right: this book wasn't going to write itself. She didn't have Tori's powers.

3

The party was in full swing by the time Cat recognized the woman in the witch costume standing next to a werewolf. Harriet Barring, the Covington English professor who had challenged the college's sponsorship of the retreat stood there, drinking Cat's wine like she'd been invited. Okay, so Cat had put a flyer up for any English department member to attend, but she really hadn't expected anyone to show up. Especially not Professor Barring. And yet, there were several members of the English department milling around. Maybe they came to see the fight that was just about to happen.

She moved toward Professor Barring to give a piece of her mind when Seth stepped in front of her. She tried to move around him, but he grabbed her arm. When she met his gaze and tried to shrug out of his grip, she saw his grin. "I'm busy."

"I know what you're about to do and it's not worth it. She came with her husband, Stephen, who's part of Tammy's writers group. You'd just make a scene and you'd be seen as the bad guy if you did. So just stay here and talk to me." Seth moved her over to the bar where he ordered her a class of chardonnay and a beer for himself. He paid for the drinks and then moved her away from the dining room where the others had been standing. "Besides, you look stunning in that outfit and I've been wanting to tell you exactly how amazing all night."

He always knew how to distract her. Cat twirled in the tulle skirt. The glitter sparkled in the low light. "I'm going to regret making a Tori costume for this. I'll never get all of the glitter out of the wood floors. But I have to admit, playing dress up is really fun."

"You should wear it at your book events. I bet your fans would get a kick out of it." He held out his beer and clinked it on her glass. "I'm glad to be home."

She studied him as he took a drink. Her heart squeezed a little at his words.

Then he lowered it and sighed at the look on her face. "I've ruined the night again, haven't I?"

She shook her head. "No, I just had this totally biting, sarcastic response that I was going to blurt out, and then I realized I'm just keeping myself in this pain. I don't want to fight with you."

"I don't want to fight either. We agreed put this aside until after the retreat, but what if we go away for a weekend? I'll have to sweet-talk Shauna into watching Sam, but I think we need to say some things to each other and see if we can get past them." He leaned over and kissed her on the cheek. "I still love you but if you don't feel the same, we need to put both of us out of this misery."

"Truce until after the retreat then?" Relieved, Cat held up her wine glass and Seth clinked his beer bottle. She kept his gaze. She wanted to tell him how she felt, but she was afraid she'd burst into tears at the words. Not a good look for someone who was supposed to be hosting a party. And there was that old song about crying at your own party. Cat seemed to remember it hadn't turned out well for the singer.

"Truce." He pointed out one of the retreat guests. The man was dressed like a vampire, but his pink dreadlocks kind of ruined the dark effect of his costume. "That Deek's a character. I don't think he shut up the entire trip from the airport. He's a surfer but now that he's here, he's thinking about coming back to do some skiing or snowboarding later this year. If he can get the time off. I didn't realize working at a bookstore was that demanding of a job. But don't ask him about it, he'll tell you more than you want to know."

"Some people like hearing about what it's like to work at a bookstore." Cat pointed to the woman next to him. "Who's the sprite again?"

"Pixie," Seth said, and then he chuckled as Cat turned toward him with a question on her face. "Yes, her name is Pixie. She's part of the California group. I think she's sweet on Deek, but he's oblivious. The sexy witch standing next to her is Cari Black. She writes witch stories too, but a hotter, adult romance version. She's had some success with self-publishing, but she's working on getting a real deal."

"A real deal?"

"Her words, not mine." Seth held up his hands to ward off the blow. "One with a big publisher. She says her folks are English professors at a local community college and keep asking her when she's going to take this career seriously."

"Is she paying her own way?" Cat watched the two women. Neither one moved from their claimed corner of the room with their wine glasses in hand. But they were watching everything and everyone. Including Deek, who had just moved from one group to another. He was the social butterfly of the group. Maybe they should move the party to the end of the week when people had a chance to feel more comfortable. Especially the introverts.

"She said she just bought a house with her writing money, so I think that's a yes. Especially since it's a house in California." Seth studied the room. "Writers are a different breed. They're all needy and wanting to be proven worthy."

"Well, thanks for that, Dr. Phil." Cat turned her attention to Seth.

His face pinked even under the white makeup he'd put on for Frankenstein. "Cat, I didn't mean you. You already have your proof. You're published."

"And so is Cari. I get so tired of us judging each other by how we make our money. Or if we make money at all. Writers are writers. A lot of the greats were seen as hacks when they were alive." She nodded to the professor and her husband. "Making walls only hurts all of us."

"I believe someone said good fences make good neighbors. Maybe Ben Franklin?" A dark-haired young man who looked like a Greek demigod broke into their conversation. He was dressed in a flowy poet shirt with no buttons closed, showing off a chest that only came from a lot of time in the gym. His leather pants completed the outfit. "Sorry for my intrusion, I wanted to introduce myself. I'm Dalton Diggs, your Covington scholarship student for the retreat. Thank you for inviting me to the pre-party. This is cool."

"Nice to meet you, Dalton." Cat held out a hand and tried not to be drawn into looking at his abs. "I'm Cat Latimer, and this is Seth Howard."

Seth looked at her for a second, then held out his own hand. "I'll be here at the retreat full time. In case you need something."

"Oh, dude, nice to know. I'm hoping to carve out some runs in the morning, if you're up to it." He looked down at the cane. "Sorry, is that part of the costume?"

"No, unfortunately, I was hurt during an assignment earlier this year." He put his arm on Dalton's shoulder and turned him toward the room. He pointed out the dreadlocked vampire. "I'm sure we can find someone to run with you. Maybe Deek's a runner."

"I'll go check. Thanks, Frankenstein dude." He pointed to his own shirt. "Do you get it? My costume? My girlfriend helped me with it. She said I'd be a hit with these writers."

"A poet? Maybe?" Cat guessed although she didn't think any of the classic poets wore leather pants.

"Dude, no." Dalton laughed like she'd told the funniest joke. He pointed to his chest. "I'm the poet. That's my real life. This is the guy on the romance covers. Fabion?"

"Fabio," Seth corrected. "Yep, that's Fabio down to the wavy hair. Of course, he was blond."

"Maybe he was photoshopped," Dalton offered as an explanation. "Anyway, I'll see you tomorrow when I move in for the week. Looking forward to the retreat."

After he'd walked away, Cat took a sip of her wine, then a second one. "He's going to be a handful. Usually, poets are introverted and shy. He's an extrovert to the core."

"True, but I heard one good thing about our friend Dalton, aka, Fabio." Seth watched as he approached Deek like they were long lost brothers.

"What was that?" Cat tried to not look at the guy's butt. It was rude. And he was way too young for her anyway. And Seth was standing next to her.

Seth took her arm and led her toward Tammy Jones dressed in an elf costume, Shauna stood next to her chatting. "He said he already has a girlfriend so I don't have to worry about him poaching mine."

"Seth, it's so good to see you." Tammy gave him a quick hug when they arrived. "You're looking stronger, well, except for that white face. If I didn't know it was makeup, I'd be suggesting you sit down right about now."

"I don't think that's a bad idea anyway," Cat said. "Let's go into the living room and chat a bit. I know you wanted to change up your session this time and hold it at the bookstore. Is that still the plan?" Cat took Tammy's arm and led her to the living room. Getting Seth off that leg without him thinking that was her plan wasn't the worst idea. "Seth, Shauna, you're part of this discussion too, so let's go. Might as well do a bit of business at this party."

Shauna took Seth's arm and nodded toward the retreating pair. "I guess we've been summoned. And no, Cat doesn't understand the purpose of parties is to avoid the business part of the retreat. But I'll give her this one. My feet are killing me in these heels."

As they got seated, Cat smiled at her friend. "Well, you're a fairy, just make them more comfortable shoes."

"That's an elf. I don't cobble shoes. I grant wishes but never my own. Or I'd be on a beach in the Caribbean enjoying some rum punch." She picked up her glass and took a sip. "Okay, maybe I do have some powers. That's a pretty strong rum punch. One good thing came out of the night. Stephen Barring just signed up for the last slot in the writers' retreat. He's checking in tomorrow."

Tammy looked shocked at the news. "That's surprising. I mean, I know he talked about attending the retreat someday, but his wife was dead set against it."

"Well." Shauna leaned in, keeping her voice low. "He told me Deek mentioned one of the California writers had bailed on the trip. Deek feels awful about it. He's told me that several times. Since she didn't get a refund, I told him it wasn't an issue. Stephen came over right when the party was getting started and asked if there was still a slot. When I said yes, he handed over his card and paid the week in full." Shauna pulled out the receipt from her pocket. "We did this before the bar opened, so he wasn't drunk at the time. So no do overs. We do have a thirty day before the session refund policy. I explained it twice."

"I'm glad for him. I think he needs to be around more writers. His wife doesn't approve of his genre. He writes high fantasy. It's really good." Tammy sipped her drink.

"I don't think Professor Barring thinks much of anything that isn't written up in one of the university journals as modern literary. She's one of those people who have to be told what's good by someone else." Cat rolled her shoulders. "I can't believe she stooped to attend our party, but if her husband's going to be a retreat guest, I suppose I need to get used to seeing her around this week."

"He said she's busy at the college with some sort of project." Shauna set her glass down and met Cat's gaze. "Maybe I should have talked to you first? I was just happy we had a full group since one of the South Cove writers cancelled."

"No, you did the right thing. I'm just going to have to be an adult and be nice to Harriet. But next week, I'm going back to hating her." Cat turned to Tammy. "Let's talk about what's going on with your bookstore session. What do you need from us?"

"First off, I want you to know that I'm really sorry about Professor Barring showing up at the party. When I talked to Stephen last week, he said she'd decided not to attend. But I didn't know he was going to sign up for the session. And now, all they're doing is fighting. I swear, he came up just to say hi and she came running over to see what we were talking about. She's so jealous. Like I'd ever sleep with some-one's husband. Especially in this town. There are no secrets here."

Cat, Seth, and Shauna exchanged a look. There was one secret, Covington's secret charter. Apparently, Tammy wasn't in the know.

"That's fine. I have to admit, I was surprised to see her. She's single handedly trying to close down the retreat." Cat saw Shauna's frown at her word choice. "Or at least cut our funding. If they keep sending us poets like Dalton, maybe not having their support wouldn't be a horrible choice. But we do need access to the library. It's one of the selling points to the retreat."

"I'm sure Miss Applebome would work something out with you. She's never thought it was fair that she didn't get a fee for the week with the students." Tammy sipped her drink and realized the rest were watching her. "What? She comes into the shop to order books a lot. We talk."

Cat nodded. "I'll consider talking to her. Especially if the hearing goes south. Having the college as a sponsor is important so I don't want to burn any bridges I'm still in the middle of crossing."

"Good imagery." Tammy leaned back in the sofa. "So let me tell you my plan for Friday's writer visit. I think you're going to love it. And, I've got some good publishing numbers on each of their specialties."

Tammy was just finishing with describing her session when loud voices came through the open living room door. Seth stood, waving the others to stay seated. "I'll go check it out. If it's our squabbling couple, I might just invite them to leave."

"Works for me." Cat rubbed her face. "The woman hates the retreat anyway. Kicking her out for fighting with her husband isn't going to change her mind about the value of the service we provide."

After Seth left the room, Tammy groaned. "Look, I'm really sorry about Harriet and Stephen. If I'd known they were going to be a problem, I would have insisted he either not bring her with him or just not show up at all. Stephen's a good guy. He teaches English as an adjunct professor at Denver's community college three nights a week. Covington won't hire him because she's on staff."

"Looks like we got the raw end of that deal. Maybe Covington can fire her and hire Stephen." Shauna sipped her drink, then noticed Cat and Tammy staring at her. "What? Did I say that out loud?"

Seth came back a few minutes later with a tray holding another round of drinks. "The fight is over and Harriet has left the building. Stephen's still here, talking to Deek, but most of the group scattered to their rooms or left when the fight started. It's after eleven, so I sent the bar and catering staff home. They'll come pack up tomorrow so if we want more drinks, we're on our own to make them. Deek and Stephen are in the dining room with a bucket of beers and the last tray of nachos and smoked sausages."

"I should go start to clean up." Shauna stood, but Seth took her empty glass and gave her a full replacement.

"No, we should sit and talk. We don't have to talk about the retreat or the college or the fate of the book world. But we don't get a lot of time to just sit and talk. Tomorrow the retreat starts. I think we should take advantage of our semi empty house for a bit." Seth sat next to Cat on the couch and put an arm around her shoulder. "What's going in Aspen Hills that I missed?"

"Besides Shauna's secret boyfriend?" Cat giggled at the look Shauna gave her. But she knew Seth was right. They needed some down time. This retreat was going to be a killer for a multitude of reasons. They had a new English professor coming from Covington on Tuesday rather than Professor Turner and his Hemmingway lecture. Cat blinked as she remembered seeing him at the bar a few hours ago dressed as Indiana Jones. She so should have gone to greet him, but she'd been upset about Barring. What was his name, Tom, Todd? Todd.

She'd call him and apologize tomorrow. She needed to update the session handout. The Friday bookstore session was changing. And tomorrow, she'd need to program some extra time for either word sprints or maybe a walk around the town and the campus for the writers. Having the session start early had changed the feel of the week. Now she just needed to make the best of the extra time they had.

THE NEXT MORNING, Cat heard someone knocking at her door. She grabbed her cellphone and saw it was already after eight. The group had stayed up talking. Finally, at twelve thirty, she'd called it. "Crap, I'm sorry, I slept in. I'll be down in a few."

The door opened and Shauna came in, closing the door behind her. "Cat, something happened."

"Is everyone okay?" Tammy had been the last to leave at midnight, but she'd called the Aspen Hill's taxi service to pick her up just before Cat had gone upstairs to bed. Shauna had stayed up to wait with her. "Tammy?"

"Tammy's fine. She texted me when she got home and thanked me for hosting the party." Shauna sat down on the bed next to Cat. "Seth went out to the barn to feed Snow and the dwarfs. He found a body."

"A body of what?" Cat rubbed her face, it was too early in the morning for games. "Look Shauna, I'm still a little hung over from last night. You should have brought up coffee if you wanted to have a talk."

"Cat, listen to me." Shauna took the phone away from her and set it on the table. "Seth found the body of a woman dressed in a zombie costume. She's dead. He thinks it's Harriet Barring."

4

C at stood looking out the kitchen window at the barn, drinking a cup of coffee. The ambulance and the cop cars had arrived through the back alley, which had direct access to the barn so they weren't using the backyard for their staging area. So far, the writers were still in bed, but she wasn't counting on that being true for much longer. Shauna had set up the dining room with a huge brunch and was cooking still more food. Cat turned to watch her put another breakfast casserole in the oven. "Are you overdoing it?"

"Anything we don't eat today, I'll repurpose tomorrow. Besides, this casserole is better warmed up the second day." She joined Cat at the sink and looked out the window. "When do you think they'll be done?"

"Well, Uncle Pete's heading this way, so probably soon. I just hope we can keep the writers from noticing what's going on. We have a bad enough reputation as the 'murder' retreat. I was hoping to get through the year without anything happening." Cat went to refill her coffee and pour a cup for her uncle. She set up a few muffins on a plate for the table as well.

He walked through the kitchen door a few minutes later. He

checked the bottom of his boots before coming farther into the kitchen. "Your grass is a little soft out there from the rain we had last week. You might want to keep people off of it until it dries off later this week."

"I'll mention it to them when we meet later. So, what about the body? Do you know who it is?" Cat hadn't ventured out to the barn since Uncle Pete has already arrived by the time she got dressed and downstairs.

"I think it's an English professor, Harriet Barring. Her face was kind of messed up but it looks basically like her. She came into the station last week complaining about her neighbor. She was tired of the weekly parties. Of course, she lives next to a rental filled with college kids. I'm not sure what she thought she was getting into when they bought in that neighborhood. Yes, it's close to the campus, but most of the professors know that they need to live a few blocks away." He nodded to the coffee. "I'm tired and my mouth is running off without me thinking about what I'm saying. Is that for me or is it Seth's?"

"Yours." She sat at the table with him. "Seth just went to let Sam out. He'll be back in a few minutes."

"I have to say again, I'm glad he's in the house with you all now. I know it didn't stop this, but at least you two were safe." He sipped his coffee and picked up a muffin. "I'm starving."

"What happened to her? Tell me she slipped and fell. Maybe she was drunk and wandered into the barn by accident." Cat frowned. "Of course, that would be bad for me, right? Since she was at my party drinking?"

"She didn't slip." Pete unwrapped the muffin. "She was beaten pretty bad."

Seth came into the kitchen and poured himself a coffee. "Hey, I've got a question. Are you sure it was Harriet? Wasn't she dressed as a witch at the party?"

"Harriet was dressed like a witch at the party. Maybe this is someone else." Cat studied Seth. He seemed to be pretty calm for finding a body this morning. She tried to process the thought that someone had died in her barn. "Of course, that's not a good idea either. My insurance agent is going to have a field day with this. Wow, I sound like a bad person."

"A wandering person dressed as a zombie? I'll be doing DNA testing but it's the Barring woman. Even if she was dressed different-ly." Uncle Pete locked gazes with Cat. "You're kidding, right?"

Shauna joined them at the table, bringing a plate of cookies. "This is weird. Harriet Barring *was* dressed as a witch at the party. Why come as one character, leave, then come back as something else?"

Seth refilled his coffee as he paced back and forth. "I can't think of a reason. Unless she wanted to come back in and have her husband not notice her. What I heard of their fight, she thought he was sleeping around."

"What fight?" Uncle Pete sighed as he pulled out his notebook. "You guys are really bad at giving me the information I need. You got to know that."

"Sorry, Pete." Seth sat at the table too. "The three of us and Tammy Jones were talking in the living room about the upcoming retreat schedule. Tammy told us she'd heard the couple fighting a lot last night. I didn't hear any fight."

"Neither did I," Cat added to Seth's story. They looked at Shauna.

She blushed, then dropped her gaze. "Okay, so I was talking to Stephen about the retreat after he'd signed up. He really enjoyed the food and wanted to know if I had done all the dishes since I cooked for the retreat. I told him I'd done some of the food, but that we'd hired a caterer, so we were going through the dishes he'd liked. Which were mostly the ones I made."

"Where's the fight in this story?" Uncle Pete glanced at his watch. "And did I hear you say that Stephen signed up for the retreat?"

"Sorry, yes, he was a last-minute addition. He's supposed to check in today, but with this, I don't know." Cat's gaze turned in the direc-tion of the barn even though she couldn't see it through the kitchen wall.

"Yes, I forgot to mention that too. As for the fight, I'm getting there. Anyway, Harriet came up, asked if I was the one sleeping with her husband since he registered for the retreat. I didn't know what to say. He stepped up and apologized and then pulled her away. I didn't win any points with her, that was certain." Shauna pushed her red hair back away from her shoulder. "I could still hear them talking. She said some pretty awful things to him."

"Okay, so that was the fight?" Uncle Pete looked up from what he was writing in his notebook.

Cat and Seth shook their heads in unison. They looked at each other and Cat pointed to Seth.

"Actually, one of the fights. Tammy said she heard one, too. And when we were in the living room, someone started yelling out in the foyer. I volunteered to take care of the problem and saw it was Harriet and Stephen. I walked over to tell them they'd have to leave, but Harriet stormed out of the front door before I even got there. Stephen apologized, Deek came over and took him into the dining room, and the rest of the attendees started leaving. Some up to their rooms, others, like Andi, left out the front door. I sent home the caterers and the bar staff. And the party was over." Seth glanced over to Cat and Shauna to see if he'd missed anything. Both women shook their heads in a silent answer.

"And no one else" —Uncle Pete looked straight at Cat— "talked to Harriet last night?"

"Why do you always look at me?" Cat held up her hand. "I swear, I didn't get in a fight with Harriet. I was with Seth, Tammy, and Shauna, then when Tammy called a taxi, I went up to my room."

"Alone?" Uncle Pete asked. "What time?"

"Twelve thirty?" Cat could feel her face heat. "And yes, alone. And I didn't leave my room until Shauna woke me up this morning."

"You're still using the security company I set you up with, right?"

Shauna nodded. "Yes, and I turned on the system after Tammy left. It's a risk since any of the writers can try to go outside and set off the alarm, but I told them they could use their cards if they wanted to leave at any time after we closed the house for the night. I called the security system this morning and told them you'd be calling later about the barn. They are expecting your call."

"Did they have any alerts last night?"

Shauna shook her head. "Not that they told me."

Uncle Pete stood, draining his coffee cup as he did. He set it down and looked at the three of them. "Okay then, just stay out of the barn until my guys leave. I know you'll need to feed tonight, so they'll be out before four."

"Sounds good." Seth stood and walked Pete to the door. "Anything we should do?"

"Just go about your normal routine. And don't tell your guests about the murder. Not until I can clear everyone from the house off the suspect list."

A strangled noise came from the kitchen door. Pixie stood there, carafe in her hand, her eyes wide. "Sorry, the coffee is all gone. Did you say there was a murder?"

AFTER AN IMPROMPTU MEETING with the writers to let them know about the murder in the barn, Cat was wiped out. She refilled her cup from the dining room carafe and looked around the room. The only one who wasn't here was Dalton. Cat assumed he'd hear about the murder from the college grapevine but if he hadn't, she'd have to go through this all again. Not the best way to start a writers' retreat.

Deek stood from where he'd been sitting by Pixie and came to refill his own cup. Instead of sitting back down, he stood close to Cat. "Don't blame yourself. I may not know you very well, but I'm pretty sure you wouldn't murder someone in your own barn right before a big event like this. South Cove has these issues too. Usually, my boss, Jill, she's all up in the investigation, to the dismay of her dude. He's the police detective for the town. Murder happens. Sometimes more than we'd like."

Cat had to stifle a laugh. Did he think she'd kill someone if there wasn't a big event or somewhere other than her barn? She pushed the thoughts aside and focused on his words. The guy was calm. Announcing that Professor Barring had been found dead had upset Pixy and Cari, but not Deek. He took it as just something that happened. She wasn't sure what made her more unnerved, his calmness or the women freaking out. "You're not disturbed at the news?"

"I mean, yes, it's a bummer that she died. I talked to Stephen a lot since I've been here and they were having problems. I mean, as a couple. I don't mean to say he killed her or anything, but they had a big fight right here at the party. I couldn't be in a relationship like that. Stephen says she's always on his case about his job in Denver." Deek studied his coffee. "I get that some people aren't meant to be married. My mom and dad were that way. But they divorced when I was a kid. I didn't have to hear them fighting, much."

"I'm divorced," Cat blurted out, surprising herself. "It wasn't pretty, but the arguing was short since I just packed and left. He let me think the worst, but he had good reasons. I think marriage is hard in the best circumstances."

"Yeah, I think you're right." He glanced around the room. "So today we're just chilling right? Maybe I can take the group on a walk around Aspen Hills? That way they're doing something and not just thinking about, well, you know."

"Hey, if you need a guide, I'm your man." Dalton Diggs came into the dining room with a large duffel bag. "Cool, breakfast is still going. Let me check into my room and grab some grub and we can head out."

"Thanks, Dalton. Stephen, Shauna will check you in at the front desk." Cat turned to the women at the table. "Deek had a great idea for the day."

After explaining the day's activities and that snacks would be available all day, but they were on their own for the other two meals, Cat left the group alone in the dining room. They all seemed a little less shocked and ready to get on with their retreat.

The front door opened and Stephen Barring walked in with a suitcase. His eyes were bloodshot. Cat wasn't sure if it was from crying or the drinking. He walked over to her. "I'm still allowed to attend the retreat, right? I paid and have my receipt right here."

"Yes, of course, but if you wanted to change it, I know we have a strict no refund policy after a certain date, but because of the circumstances..." Cat paused, she was doing this all wrong. She started over. "Stephen, I'm so sorry for your loss."

"Thanks. But if it's okay, I'd rather be here. The house is too quiet." He nodded to where Shauna and Dalton stood at the front desk. "Do I check in over there?"

After the men had dropped their bags into their rooms, the writers group left. Cat had made an offer for a writing sprint session in the living room starting at seven and they'd all been excited for it. Or at least they were now. Cat thought from the tired look on Pixie's face, she might just choose to turn in early.

Cat brought the last of the breakfast dishes from the dining room into the kitchen. Seth was eating at the table and Shauna stood at the sink, washing dishes. "Here's the last of them. I think both Dalton and Stephen ate before they left on the walkabout."

"I can't believe that poor man is going to work on writing this week." Shauna took the dishes from Cat. "If it was me who lost a spouse, I'd be a total mess."

"If you actually loved them," Seth added, taking a break from his waffles covered with what smelled and looked like huckleberry sauce. Cat wanted some even though she'd eaten with the writers that morning while she broke the news.

"That's cold," Shauna said, then she shrugged. "But you have a point. At least Pete knows where Stephen's at if he needs to interview him."

"Yeah, but aren't there a lot of arrangements to make? Like for the funeral and such?" Cat filled a cup with coffee and sat down, dipping her finger into the pool of syrup on Seth's plate.

He waved his fork at her. "Stop that. If you want a waffle, get your own. There's some in the oven."

"I ate before. I just wanted a taste." Cat licked the syrup from her finger. "Anyway, do you think his attending makes him look more or less like the killer?"

"He could just not want to be in the house where they had their lives, like he told me." Shauna shrugged as she dried off her hands with a towel. "It would be hard to be in a house with all her stuff there. Maybe he's just in denial."

"If he did kill her, he's stone cold. Of course, if he didn't, he seems a little cold about the whole thing too." Seth took his plate to the sink and washed it, setting it on the rack after rinsing to dry. "I beginning to think Pete's right about having someone here during retreat days. I'm going to block off my schedule for the full week. I've got enough work around here to keep me busy and you guys won't be alone with the grieving husband-slash- maybe-killer guy."

"You and Uncle Pete worry too much," Cat said, but a part of her was glad Seth would be here. No matter what happened between them, she could always count on him. And that was enough for today. "I'm heading upstairs to work. The writers will be back after lunch but we're not doing anything formal until seven when we'll be in the living room."

"Okay, I've got sandwich stuff in the fridge for lunch. I was going to ride Snow this afternoon, but it depends on when the barn is released." Shauna stared out the window toward the barn. "Dinner will be at five. I've got a shepherd's pie ready to put in the oven. Pete might drop in. I know it's not typical Sunday dinner, but we don't usually have a big Saturday night party either."

"Your food is amazing no matter what night it is." Seth pulled on his coat. "I'm going out to check on the progress at the barn. I'm sure Snow wants to be let out into the pasture by now."

Cat refilled her coffee and grabbed a couple of cookies. Then she left the kitchen. No matter what happened, they were a team. And she was going to do her best to keep it that way. Their friendship was too precious for her to lose. Especially after the stark reminder they'd gotten that morning about how fleeting life was at times.

Harriet would never have the chance to learn that lesson.

5

As Cat had predicted, Pixie bowed out of the writing sprints. But Dalton, Deek, Stephen, and Cari were all already on their laptops writing when Cat came into the room with her own. She opened the credenza that held all the writing retreat supplies in the living room including paper, pens, and a large digital timer. Then she pulled out a white board. She had added this a few sessions ago to keep a running total of words each participant wrote during retreat week. During sprints, she added the word totals, but each writer was encouraged to add their non-sprint time words for each day as well, to keep a record of the total word count.

"Before we start, we have a poet in our group this week. So, Dalton, if we kept word counts for you, it might make the totals look uneven. Do you want to keep track of your time spent creating rather than words?" Shauna had already set up a grid with everyone's name on the top, including Cat's, and the days of the week with two slots. One for sprints, one for daily totals. Cat set out different colored markers for the writers to use.

Dalton closed his laptop. "So, do you have to report anything back to the English department on what I write this week?"

"No. One, what and how much you write is your decision. If you totally blew off the retreat, I'd probably mention it, but you're here and ready to work. That's all that matters." Cat wasn't sure why Dalton was worried. She'd never had an issue with any of her Covington writers actually participating in the retreat. Of course, there was always the first time.

"Butt in chair time, dude." Deek grinned at Dalton. "That's the magic sauce from what I read of successful authors."

"I don't mean I won't be participating or not putting my butt in my chair." Dalton reached over and tapped Deek on the shoulder with his fist. Cat could see a bromance brewing between the two men. "I just don't want you telling them what I'm actually working on. I have a rep and a scholarship in poetry."

"What are you working on, Dalton?" Cari turned to focus on him, apparently curious about his answer.

"I'm writing a thriller with a vampire elite tactical team that's going after a bad seed." Dalton's words came out so fast, Cat had to let it set a minute to let the meaning settle.

"That sounds amazing," she said after a few seconds when she realized the true meaning of why he didn't want the college to know. "But you're afraid some professors won't think of it as worthy."

Dalton nodded, his face red. "They can't know."

The room was quiet for a minute, then Stephen spoke. "My wife was one of the true believers in literary fiction. If it didn't meet her definition of art, it wasn't worth pursuing. I'm sure you're an excellent poet, Dalton, but you shouldn't have to hide your other creations, just because you think you'll be judged on them. You'll find out in this world what you think about what you do matters a lot more than what anyone else in the world thinks. Even those you care about."

"Well said, Stephen." Cat smiled at him, then turned back to the group. "Your secret's safe with us. You'll need to let Pixie know not to out you in public, but there will be no report going from the retreat back to the college, except on your participation. And you're already acing that in my eyes."

～

THE NEXT MORNING, Cat woke early and practiced some yoga in her room as she thought about the last few days. The retreat had started out well enough. But then Harriet had kind of crashed the party and then wound up dead in Cat's barn. She wondered at the significance of changing her clothes from the witch costume she'd worn at the party into the zombie costume she'd been found in the barn wearing. Maybe it was the same costume with some tweaks. Harriet couldn't have thought she could get away with coming back into the party in a different outfit to spy on her husband, could she? According to Seth, the party had wound down anyway by the time she'd stormed out, so it would have been over when she came back in the new outfit.

As Cat tried to make sense of the murder, nothing fit together, so she cleared her mind and finished off her stretching, only focusing on her breath and the positions she was trying to get her body to make. Shauna had been pushing Cat to at least try yoga and she had to admit, she felt great when she was done. She just felt like an idiot when she was doing it. Especially in the classes that Shauna drug her to with all the young co-eds who could bend in ways Cat didn't yet.

She pushed away the thoughts about who murdered Evil Harriet and got ready for her day. The first thing she needed to do was a quick breakfast meeting with the writers. She used to do this discussion on Sunday night, but a lot of times, people didn't know what they wanted out of the retreat. Now, she discussed it on Monday before breakfast and asked the writers to turn in a plan by the end of the day. That way, if she needed to make any changes to the retreat schedule, she could before the week was over.

She stopped by the kitchen to chat with Shauna before she met the writers at eight. "Good morning. You'll be happy to know I actually practiced yoga poses this morning, just like you taught me."

"Maybe you should set up a DVR in your room and I could lend you my workouts. That way, you don't get bored with one routine, and you can challenge yourself." Shauna came over and sat next to her at the table. "How'd sprinting go last night?"

"Good. We have a thriller writer we weren't counting on." Cat broke open a still warm muffin and watched the steam come out until she put a bit of butter into the opening.

"Stephen? Didn't he write paranormal? I'm trying to remember what Tammy said." Shauna grabbed a muffin as well, but she didn't drown it in butter like Cat did.

"High fantasy. Like *Lord of the Rings*? No, this isn't Stephen, it's Dalton. Our poet has a secret vampire novel in progress, but he doesn't want the college to find out."

"Seriously? That's a twist I didn't see coming. I thought he might be a problem during the retreat, but it sounds like he'll fit right in with Deek and the others." Shauna took a bite of the muffin. "There's not too much cinnamon in these, are there?"

"You're kidding, right? It tastes like the cinnamon sugar toast I used to make as a kid. Spot on." She finished the first half of her muffin. "I'm glad he told us. It's hard to be secretly writing what you are drawn to. That happened to me at first. Michael was mortified I sent my witch young adult to the agent rather than the dry dissertation novel where I'd tried to be so clever with word choices and personal dynamics. That thing is still on my hard drive. I might delete it on my death bed, just to make sure it never gets published."

"Pete called earlier to apologize for missing Sunday dinner. He said the case was keeping him busy, but he wouldn't expand. In fact, he laughed when I asked. He said I was hanging out with you too much." Shauna grinned as she stood to check the contents of the oven, which from the smell, held chocolate chip cookies. "I told him that was a compliment, but you know Pete. He just laughed again."

Cat sighed as she used her forefinger to pick up the last crumbs from the muffin. She could just get another one, but one wasn't enough and two was way too many. "I wish he trusted my judgment on these things. I haven't done anything stupid since I stopped hanging out at the bar where you bartended in California. And that was all about my choice of men."

"I could have told you that Tommy was a bad idea. He went through women like paper plates," Shauna reminded Cat.

"No judgment from you. When we met, you were dating that

actor guy. What was his name, George with a J?" Cat pointed out. "He used to stand you up for dates for practice readings with his drama group."

"He was focused on learning the craft." Shauna shook her shoulders like she was pushing off a bad memory. "I should have known that I wasn't his priority when he took a call from one of the girls in his class on our first date. She had news about a possible casting call, and they talked most of the dinner. I was about to get up and leave when he finally noticed I was uncomfortable and ended the conversation. I can't believe I put up with him for six months."

"You dated him almost a year," Cat pointed out as she checked the clock. "But now you're dating Mr. Secret and much better off. Unless Jeorge has found you in Colorado? Maybe he's here doing community theater?"

"It's not Jeorge." Shauna pinked as she stood and went to the counter to take out a mixing bowl. "And you're going to be late for your goal setting talk."

"And you're avoiding the conversation about your new beau." Cat laughed as she grabbed the folder with the forms and her coffee cup. "I'll find out who it is. Like you pointed out earlier, I'm good at sleuthing."

"Correction, you're good at snooping. There's a difference." Shauna measured ingredients into the blue bowl she'd grabbed. From what Cat could see, it was cookies, or a cake, or some other type of baked goods. All she knew was it would be yummy.

"Don't be a hater." Cat backed out of the kitchen and almost ran into Seth on his way in. "Oh, good morning."

"Hey, beautiful. Looks like you're on your way to your writer friends. Everything okay this morning?" He locked her gaze with his deep blue eyes.

Cat felt the intensity of the stare through her entire body. He acted like he still loved her, but could she trust him not to take off again? When he'd put off the wedding, he'd hurt her. And she'd hurt him when she'd married Michael. Maybe they were just destined to dodge and weave a real relationship in this life. When she was ready, he wasn't. When he was ready, she wasn't. Biting her bottom lip, she blinked first. "Everything's fine. We're doing an opening exercise before breakfast, then heading to the library. We should be able to walk to campus since the weather is supposed to be nice."

"Yeah, this holds up and you won't need a driver until Saturday when we go for dinner." Seth squeezed her arm. "I won't keep you. Just wanted to say good morning. Sam's missing you too. Maybe this afternoon if you have some time, you could stop by the apartment and see him."

"I might." Cat saw the brief disappointment cover Seth's face, then he smiled again. "I'm trying to get that book done."

"I know, you're busy. Retreat weeks always are. You're welcome anytime. I wonder what Shauna has planned for breakfast." He stepped around her and went into the kitchen, leaving her alone in the hallway.

She swallowed and stood there a minute, collecting her thoughts. She needed to get their relationship status cleared up but they'd agreed to leave it alone until after the retreat. Seven more days and the house would be theirs again. Then she and Seth would sit down and talk. Hopefully, they'd both be happy with the results.

She headed to the dining room and counted heads. Four people sat around the table. She looked closer and saw Stephen was missing. She set the folder down and refilled her coffee cup. "Does anyone know where Stephen is this morning?"

"I know he was awake because I saw him and Dalton coming back in the house from running when I came down for coffee," Pixie offered. "That was about seven. I'm a pretty early riser, so I took my laptop into the living room and wrote. I hope that was okay."

"That's fine. In fact, there are several approved writing spots in the house. The east wing is still being renovated so that's off limits. Seth has his dog in that area, so please don't open the door that has the Employees Only sign taped on it. But down that hall is also a small den with a library of writing and local history books available for your use. It has a desk and a writing chair in there."

Deek held up his hand. "Dibs."

"Typically, one person grabs it and claims it early, so unless someone decides to join you, I don't mind. There's also the living room where we had sprints last night. Most of our meetings and group events like tomorrow's session from Professor Lancaster will occur in there. Of course, you can use your room on the second floor, but all rooms on the third floor are off limits. My office is up there so if you can't find me, I'll probably be in there. You can come in to chat if you need to, just knock first."

She looked around the table. "There's also an attic on the fourth floor where we've set up several different types of seating. You can hold a group meeting up there if someone's in the living room. Or here if you don't mind being around the snacks. And there's also the front porch. The back yard has several different seating areas as well. The grounds a little soft and muddy because of the recent rain, so you might not want to venture too far. The barn isn't off limits, but Shauna has her horse stabled there and we have several cats out there."

"I saw one in the living room this morning. She was beautiful," Pixie said.

"That's Angelica. She comes in when she feels the need for human companionship, but I think her kittens like Snow better than us." Cat heard a noise and looked up to see Stephen coming into the room. "Good morning."

"Sorry, I went for a run, then showered and got lost in a book. It's crazy. It's like there isn't an outside world while I'm here. I know that isn't true, but it's nice putting aside all the drama going on for a bit." He filled a cup and sat down at the table. "I apologize for my lateness."

"No problem. We were just going over house rules. The group can catch you up. I was just going to mention the small gym we have in the basement. The doorway is labeled and there's weights along with a treadmill and a rowing machine, just in case the weather doesn't allow for a run. Although, it's supposed to be really nice this week." Cat paused as she looked over her notes. "Oh, and one more place to write. You were all, except Dalton, given temporary passes to get you into the Covington Library this week. After your orientation this morning, you have free range of the library as well. So if you'd rather write there, it's available. And if you check out any books, you can leave them at the front desk here on Sunday before you leave and we'll return them."

"Sounds like a busy week." Cari stood and got a glass of orange juice. "I looked over our schedule and there's not a session for Thursday. Is that right?"

"It's a free day for you to either relax or focus on what you want to finish before the end of the retreat. Friday night, we'll get together and review what we got done, but before we can do that, I have an exercise for you to do. Please turn them into the basket on the front desk by five today. That way, if we have any special requests, we can adjust the retreat to what you need from us." Cat handed out the papers. "I'll do my goal list as well since I'll be working this week too. I have a rapidly upcoming deadline."

Pixie raised her hand. "Can I get one of those? Maybe from a big New York publishing house?"

The group laughed and she looked around the table. "Dudes, I was totally serious."

"I can't get you a contract so you have a deadline, but we can talk about the state of the publishing world in our Wednesday session with me. And, I can teach you how to make your own deadlines. If you have other questions like that, please add them to this planning sheet. I don't want to miss anything. And remember, this is your retreat. So let me know how we can mold it to what you need." Cat set down the planner sheet she'd handed out. "Any questions?"

Five heads shook.

"Okay then, if you haven't gotten something to eat, please make yourself at home. Otherwise, let's dig in. I'm starving and Shauna's an excellent cook. I'm sorry if you gain weight this week, but I can promise you won't go hungry." Cat stood and went to fill a plate for herself. Most of the breakfast hours, the writers would have the room for their own, but she wanted to make sure they knew she was approachable and here if they needed something.

The room had cleared out about ten and Cat reminded everyone they had a meeting with Miss Applebome at eleven. They'd need to leave at twenty till to not be late, and the head librarian didn't approve of tardiness. A fact Cat had learned early in her college years. Miss Applebome ran the Covington library with an iron fist, and she was still twerked at the fact that Cat had "borrowed" a book a few years ago without checking it out.

Cat had learned the hard way that Covington's library was as secure as Fort Knox and probably held as many secrets.

6

Cat delivered the writers to the first-floor conference room precisely at ten fifty-five. Miss Applebome stood waiting. A middle-aged woman with a gray topknot, she filled the stereotype to a T. She nodded her approval. Too early and the group might have been too comfortable in the space. Any later and the librarian would have considered them late. She had a fine line of what was acceptable, and Cat tried hard to stay on her good side.

"Hey, Librarian Extraordinaire, I haven't seen you for a few weeks. Did you change the way you fix your hair?" Dalton Diggs stopped at the doorway and smiled at Miss Applebome. "You look amazing."

To Cat's surprise, a tinge of pink flooded the woman's cheeks.

"Dalton, go sit down, or you can be excused from this session, since you're very aware of the library and its different uses." Miss Applebome's tone was a little higher than normal.

"I'd rather sit in, if you don't mind. I'm sure I've forgotten a lot about the library since our original freshman orientation. Besides, I enjoy hearing you talk about the history of the Covington Library. Are you going to tell them about the Hemmingway section? I can't believe we got his personal papers here. What a coup for you!" Dalton nodded and went in to sit in the front row.

The boy had flirting skills, that was obvious. Cat turned to leave but Miss Applebome stopped her.

"I just wanted to let you know how much the library appreciated the gift from Michael's estate. We'll be able to upgrade not only the economics section of the library but several others as well. And have room left for fiction acquisitions for this and a few years to come. It was quite generous of you." The librarian looked surprised that her words had come out so nice. If you were choosing words to describe Miss Applebome, "nice" wasn't on the list.

Cat wasn't sure what gift she was talking about, but she'd turned over part of her ex-husband's estate to his lawyer since she wasn't sure the money was totally legally obtained. Michael had friends and clients who had questionable income sources. She'd left anything that hadn't been from life insurance or other traceable sources in a trust to be donated when the lawyer could make sure it wasn't going to need to be returned. She had a letter from the lawyer that she hadn't opened on her desk. Apparently, he'd started doling out the funds.

"Michael would have wanted to support Covington and the library as much as possible. He loved working here." Cat was getting better at knowing what to say. When Michael had died, they'd already been divorced for several years. Yet here at Covington, she was treated as his widow rather than an ex-wife. "I'm glad you can find use for the donation."

"Libraries are often the first line of cuts when university presidents have to trim the budget. Books are what keeps us thinking and understanding each other. And the library is the heart of the university. Administration just doesn't understand that. They'd rather make sure the athletic departments are overfunded than 'waste' money on books and resources." Miss Applebome patted Cat's arm. "It's people like you, people who understand and have a love of learning, that truly understand what we do here. The gift might have been in Michael's name, but I know you were the one who determined that the library would get the money. So thank you."

Cat nodded, unable to speak. She did believe in lifelong learning, but she didn't know the librarian had realized that. Or that she saw Cat as anything but Michael's ex-wife. Finally, she croaked out a short, "Thank you." Then she turned and left the building.

The writers would attend the library meeting, then find somewhere to have lunch. Dalton had listed off most of the local restaurants as they walked to the library. Then they were free to return to the library for research or writing time and wouldn't be expected back at the house until after dinner for a "come as you are" writing sprint session. She had a free afternoon.

Instead of going home and opening that letter, she decided to visit her uncle. Maybe he had news on the murder investigation. She'd like to know who had decided to take out a Covington professor in her barn. Maybe it was tied to the college's special student roster.

No one was at the front desk when Cat entered the police station, so she walked straight to her uncle's office. He was on the phone, but he saw her and held up a finger. She stood in the doorway, waiting for him to invite her in or tell her to go wait in the lobby. It was kind of a limbo land. Not in his office, but not out either. Kind of like how she'd felt about Michael and their marriage. He'd set up a situation where she'd thought he was cheating on her. And then he hadn't fought the divorce. Or fought for her to stay.

At the time, she'd been too mad to question his actions, but later, she'd found out he'd been trying to protect her. He'd gotten in too deep with something and been killed. On paper, his death was still ruled an accident, but she'd been told that another "court of justice" had found his murderer and had killed him. She still wasn't sure what she thought about all of it. So she tried not to examine it closely.

"Can I help you?" a woman asked from behind her.

Cat turned and saw a woman with a cup of coffee standing there. "I'm just waiting for my uncle. No one was at the desk."

"Sorry, that was my bad. I went to get Pete, I mean, Chief Edwards a fresh cup of coffee. I'm Penelope. I'm the new administration coordinator."

"Catherine Latimer, but you can call me Cat." She reached out a hand. Uncle Pete had mentioned he'd hired someone to take over the clerical duties of the station, but he hadn't mentioned she was a knockout. "Do people call you Penny?"

"Not if they want to live." Penelope went into the office and dropped off the cup just as Uncle Pete got off the call. She smiled at him. "You have a visitor."

"I see that. Come on in, Cat. You've met Penelope?" He stood as Cat walked in the office.

Cat looked between Uncle Pete and Penelope and nodded. "I remember you mentioning you had a new hire. So nice to meet you. Have you worked in law enforcement before?"

"Heavens no. I worked for a lawyer out of Denver before I decided to get out of the city. Pete was nice enough to ignore my lack of law enforcement background and give me a shot." She started to leave. "I better get back to the front. Officer Grant is on a break and we've already had one unauthorized walk in."

Cat waited for her to leave and shut the door behind her. "Penelope's very pretty."

"I guess." Her uncle sat down and didn't meet her gaze. "She's very good at her job. She cleaned out that file cabinet in less than a week. I've been working on it for years."

"Does Shirley know you have a new employee?" Cat watched as the red took over his face.

"No, and before you say anything, I'm planning on telling her this week. I just wanted to see if Penelope would even work out before I caused any waves with Shirley." Uncle Pete leaned forward and stared at her. "Now don't you be doing anything stupid. I will tell her."

"Not my circus, not my monkey." Cat leaned back in the chair. "So, anything on the murder investigation I should know?"

"No, and no. I'm not talking to you about it." Uncle Pete moved a pile of files to the side of his desk.

"That seems to be your answer for everything, not talking about it." Cat held up a hand before he could respond. "Sorry, that was uncalled for. I'm just a little off. The library got a check from Michael's estate."

"So the family must have come to an agreement?" Uncle Pete

knew about the special circumstances around Covington College and Aspen Hills. Basically, the college was originally chartered for the sole purpose of being somewhere safe that mob families could send their children to get a college degree without fear of reprisal from any other family. Covington and by location, Aspen Hills, was protected by the charter. No mob business was supposed to happen at the college or in the town. A family leader had gone outside the rule book in the Michael situation. And they'd paid for their rule breaking with the most severe punishment available.

"I guess. I know I told Dante to keep me out of the discussion about the money, but I thought he might let me know when it was over. At least the library is benefiting from the situation. Maybe he's not in town." Cat chose a grape lollipop out of the jar on Uncle Pete's desk. She'd been upset since Miss Applebome had told her about the donation. Even though Michael had been gone now for years. And they'd been divorced for longer than that. What was it about relationships that kept giving you a sucker punch?

"Look, if you want, I'll reach out to Mr. Cornelio and see what's going on. He arrived in town late last week. His team reported to the station as soon as they arrived as per the covenant. I'm surprised he hasn't reached out to you for coffee. I know the two of you are friends." Her uncle watched her face as she took in the news. What he didn't say was he didn't like the fact she was friends with Dante, who was now head of one of the biggest mob families in the country.

"I think I was pretty clear the last time we talked that all we were was friends. So maybe he's still mad about that." Cat got up and stretched. "Well, if you aren't going to give me any information about Professor Barring's murder, I'm heading back to the house. Shauna was making grilled cheese for lunch."

"Cat, just be careful. From what I can see, there's at least one suspect for the murder attending your retreat. I know I cleared everyone with a background check, but Stephen Barring and his wife were serial domestic violence calls. I've heard rumors about an improper relationship between her and at least one student. Dalton Diggs' name has come up several times as the possible student, although no one had seen anything but some heavy flirting between the two. The husband signs up for the retreat right before his wife was killed and then decides to continue to attend? He's not acting the part of grieving widower well."

"We all grieve in our own ways." Cat thought about Stephen's answer when she'd asked the same question, if he was sure he wanted to do this now. "He told me that it was better than being in their house."

Uncle Pete tapped his pen on the table. "Now that I can understand. After your aunt died, I spent a lot of nights on that couch over there. I didn't want to go home to a bed that was going to be empty forever."

"You'll tell me if you find more evidence, right?" Cat paused at the door. "I don't want anyone else to be in danger."

"I'll shut your retreat down if I think one of the writers is the killer. Don't worry, I'm keeping a close eye on all of you."

After she left the station, she turned toward home. She wanted to be sitting in the kitchen, eating grilled cheese, and laughing with Shauna and Seth. Not thinking about death and reasons behind a killing.

When she got home, Shauna took a plate out of the oven and set it in front of her at the table. "I was expecting you back fifteen minutes ago."

"I stopped to talk to Uncle Pete." She didn't make eye contact with either Shauna or Seth and she could feel their gazes on her. "Nothing to be worried about. I was just checking in on the investigation."

"I bet Pete loved that. How many times has he told you to not Nancy Drew a case?" Seth got up and poured himself a glass of milk. "Cat, I saw the body. Whoever killed Harriet Barring was angry. The body was beat up. I don't know if that was the cause of death, but she looked a lot like the zombie she was dressed up as."

"That's what's bothering me. She was dressed as a witch at the party. Why would she be in a zombie costume when she was found?" Cat took a bite of her sandwich, the gooey cheese still hot. "Did anyone see a zombie at the party?"

"A couple." Shauna nodded. "I talked to one of them. That professor doing the Covington seminar tomorrow. He was dressed as an Indiana Jones wannabe but his wife was in a zombie costume. Not that it was a good costume, just a ripped-up t-shirt and some over-sized dirty jeans. She did have on some nice earrings, which a true zombie would have lost."

"That's right. I talked to him before we all went to the living room to meet with Tammy. We talked briefly about his session tomorrow." Cat remembered that Professor Lancaster had been standing by the wall, watching but not really talking to anyone. "He seemed uncom-fortable being there. I bet he was worried about Harriet and her snitching on him with the rest of the English department."

"You all are a little touchy about what you write, aren't you?" Shauna finished her sandwich and stood to put the plate in the dish-washer. "You make it sound like a crime to be seen at our sordid writ-ers' retreat."

"For literary writers, it is." Cat set her sandwich down. "When I taught at Covington, my next step would have been to publish a book. And they didn't want to hear about the Tori series. They wanted a serious piece of literature, like a modern take on Hemingway or Tolstoy. A teenage witch going to a school for creatures, that wasn't real writing. Michael was horrified when he found out I sent that book to the agent. And yet, that was the book that sold and set up this author career. A book and series I love to write."

"It's kind of like the difference in being a handyman and a general contractor," Seth put in. "My buddies always tease me that I'm wasting my time building decks and remodeling houses. But I like working on one project at a time. I get to help people out that don't have the money to hire someone to build a completely new house for them."

Cat was surprised that Seth understood. But then she realized, he had always understood her. She was the one who'd thought she wanted to teach at the university level. He'd known her true love had been story, even back in high school.

"Well, I'm going to take Snow out for a jaunt at the arena while the writers are gone. I'll be back by five and have dinner on the table by six, if that will work." Shauna wiped her hands on a towel and looked around at the kitchen. "We've got more than enough treats for today and I'm planning on baking again tomorrow."

"Have fun." Cat watched as Seth stood as well. "Where are you going?"

"I'm going to paint on the third floor. I think we might have more guest rooms for your January retreat if I don't run into any issues between now and then." He put his plate in the dishwasher. "Thanks for the grub, Shauna. Yummy as usual."

"You're most welcome." Shauna went to the door and pulled on her coat as Seth disappeared into the hallway outside the kitchen. She turned to Cat as she grabbed the keys to the truck. "What are your plans?"

"I'm going upstairs to work. I've got to hit this deadline." Cat held up her sandwich. "Just as soon as I finish this."

When she was alone in the kitchen, she felt a chill. The house was almost totally empty. Seth was in the other wing and he'd probably taken Sam with him upstairs to paint. She could go look for one of the cats, but instead, she finished her sandwich, putting the plate into the dishwasher. She watched Shauna walk out to the barn. Everyone was going on with life like nothing had happened.

So why was she so focused on a murder of a woman she hadn't even liked?

7

Cat flipped through the goal sheets she'd received from the retreat guests. Dalton was the most optimistic. He wanted to get thirty thousand words in between today and Saturday. She might have to temper his enthusiasm a bit tonight, but she'd add their word count goals to the whiteboard before they got together and maybe he'd lower his goal count himself. Stephen had the least number of words to goal. She didn't know if he was expecting grief to hit and distract him or if he was always negative about his projected word count.

She'd found that sometimes the Covington students had been brainwashed by the image of the struggling writer. Locked up in the garret, writing each word like it was made of gold or written in blood. Self-taught writers didn't know that they weren't supposed to hit three or even four thousand words a day. So they did. Now, the words tended to need a little more editing, but they got the story down. Then they could word craft it during the editing process. She made a note to talk to Shauna about holding an editing-focused session for past attendees. Maybe they could do it as a second session each month.

Or, she thought, scribbling the idea down, if they had the rooms available in January, they could run two sessions at the same time. One for writing words and the second one for editing. She'd have to add more sessions to the week, but each night, the entire group could get together to sprint. Some would be editing. Some writing. And maybe even some brainstorming time. She'd have to ask if anyone needed some for this session. The time they riffed on cozy mystery titles had been really fun.

Writing should be fun, she mused as she continued to review the goal sheets, making notes in her own planner to talk to each guest about different things as she went. Harriet Barring had considered writing a chore. A job. And worse, a calling that only the talented few could be indoctrinated into the cult of publishing.

Cat would put her faith in hard work over talent any day. Especially if the writer was willing to change and grow as they put in the work. Satisfied with the goal sheets, she slipped them back in the folder and set the folder near her laptop so she'd remember to take them down for the writing sprint session later.

Then she booted up her desktop computer. She should check email and see if she had anything pressing, but the idea of finding the fun in writing had made her think of a scene between Tori's sorority sisters and the coven members. And Tori in the middle trying to counter spell and keep her human friends from waking up with green hair and enough extra pounds on the cheerleaders to keep them from fitting into their uniforms on game day.

She'd just sent an exhausted but happy Tori to watch the football game with at least one of her coven friends who had seen the error in her ways when a knock sounded at her office door. She scribbled a note about missing one curse and having a live mascot run onto the field as she called out a short, "Come in."

"Hey, sorry to bother you, but if you're going to eat before the sprinting session tonight, you need to come down." Shauna came in with a dish pan and started filling it with coffee cups and empty plates. "The writing must be going well."

Cat stretched and checked the clock. "Wow, it's already five thirty? The writing was going amazing. I'm just going to send this to the cloud so I can continue it during the session. And, I had an idea about January's session I want to run by you and Seth."

"Well, it will have to be just me. Seth stopped in and told me he was meeting one of his friends for dinner. They're in town for the day." Shauna watched Cat turn and work on the computer. "Don't be upset. You know he's not going to leave again. He promised."

"He left last time because someone needed him. I'm not upset, but I swear, I don't understand the man at all. Anyway, I'm done here. Let's go eat and I can tell you my amazing idea." Cat shut her computer down and saw her reflection in the darkened screen. She smiled into the screen before she turned around. She might as well look like she wasn't worried. *Turn that frown upside down.* That had been one of her mom's favorite sayings when Cat was growing up.

The frown returned when she saw the pile of dishes in the dishpan Shauna was holding. "You don't have to clean up after me. I would have done it."

"You're writing. I don't mind doing my part. You were kind enough to help with dishes when I was working on the last cookbook. Tons and tons of dishes." Shauna held the door open for Cat to walk out with her laptop, her planner, and the goal sheet folder. "I'm just paying you back."

"I also got to eat your test recipes, remember? When are you starting the next cookbook?" She followed Shauna down the stairs.

"I sent some ideas over to my editor but I haven't heard back. If I don't hear anything soon, I'm going to start working on the Warm Springs Writers Retreat cookbook. That way we can get all these brunch recipes down and in one spot. And when one of the writers emails me for a recipe, I can send them the link to the cookbook." Shauna laughed as they hit the landing for the second floor. The hallway with the writers' rooms was empty and quiet.

"No one's back yet?" Cat asked.

Shauna shook her head. "Not a one. But it's only Monday. They're still all getting to know each other and not focusing on the work they want to get done."

"Three of them already know each other," Cat reminded her.

"Sometimes having a group come together isn't as effective in their development. They see it as a vacation, not a work event."

"Truly, it is a vacation. Only freaks like you think of a writing retreat as a work event," Shauna teased as they continued down the stairs.

"There's a name for freaks like me: successful authors," Cat shot back as they made their way into the kitchen to continue the conversation over dinner.

PROFESSOR LANCASTER ARRIVED PROMPTLY at nine thirty to prepare for his ten o'clock lecture. Cat met him at the door, then took him to the dining room for some coffee and treats. "I really appreciate you coming to the session this month. I know Professor Turner was disappointed that I asked you to lecture, but I have a poetry student in my group this month and wanted to give him something he could use rather than a study of story."

"Studying story is valid for both the prose and the poetry student, but I'm pleased you asked me. I haven't had the opportunity to lecture on word choice and origins since I quit teaching at the Denver Community College a few years ago. I keep submitting it as an optional class here at Covington, but I'm afraid the course contact isn't being taken seriously versus the study of Hemingway or Shakespeare."

"Sometimes we need to try new things and bring a bit of life into our plans, don't you think?" Cat poured the coffee, then sat at the table next to him. "I'm trying to recall but I don't think you were on staff when I taught at Covington. As a junior professor, I only taught the entry level classes, then I left the area."

"I've heard the stories. You were married to the great economist, Michael Latimer, if I've heard right. And you left a big hole to fill for your replacement, which was me. Everyone loved your classes." He sipped his coffee as he watched her reaction.

"Oh, I didn't know that's when you started. Thank you for taking over in the middle of a term. The dean was furious at me, but I couldn't stay for, well, personal reasons." She held out a hand. "I'm Cat, by the way. Thank you for coming to our party on Saturday. I'm sorry we didn't have more time to chat."

"Thank you for inviting me. I really enjoyed myself. I'm a bit of an introvert but I love watching people. Fodder for the work, right?" He glanced around the room filled with sweets and treats. "Call me Todd. I have to say, your new gig is much better stocked than the school's employee dining room. How do you stay so skinny?"

"My writing office is on the third floor. So lots of steps. And I like to run." Cat leaned against her chair. The change in professors for the Covington section was going to work out fine. Todd was personable, intelligent, and easy to talk to with no apparent quirks they'd need to work around. "In January, we're going to be expanding our sessions and I'd love to have you come back and talk then too. I'll pay you for your time. As it stands, Professor Turner is paid by the college as part of our contract. For this session, you'll be getting paid for your time by the college, but if I ask you back in January, I'll foot that bill."

"Sounds lovely. I've missed having extra money when I stopped doing the community college work. I thought the raise from associate professor to professor would have been a bit more. I don't miss the drive to Denver three nights a week." He finished his coffee. "Shall we get set up? I like to see where I'll be speaking, if you don't mind. And if you have any adjustments to the discussion you'd like to make, we can talk after the session."

"Sounds perfect. Thank you again." She stood and headed to the living room. "Follow me."

After she got Professor Lancaster settled in the room, she left him alone to gather his thoughts and went to the kitchen to get a water bottle. Shauna was at the counter, making what smelled like cinnamon roll dough. "Hey, our new professor is here and he's game to start coming monthly when we start up this new process with two sessions going at once."

"If we start up the new process. You said we were going to talk to Seth first and now you're hiring professors to give talks? Unless you're replacing Professor Turner with him. That I'm all for. That man can put to sleep a caffeinated colicky baby."

Cat giggled at the imagery. "He means well." She paused as she refilled her coffee cup. "Wait, have you been listening in on Turner's lectures?"

"Once or twice. I thought it might be helpful with the cookbook writing, and it was, because all I did the entire hour was think about the food I could be making instead of listening to him." She put the last roll into the pan and then covered it with foil and put it in the fridge. "Those are for tomorrow. So this new professor, you think he'll work out for the editing session?"

They talked a few minutes about the possible change and then Cat jumped up. "I better go introduce him so he feels welcome. We can finish this over lunch. Will Seth be here?"

"I think so, but maybe you should ask him yourself. You two need to actually talk to each other to work on whatever this problem is between the two of you." Shauna went over to her desk and pulled out a clipboard. "I can't be used as a telegram service this week. I've got things to do."

Shauna headed out the door and Cat followed her. They parted ways at the stairs. Shauna was heading up to do some light house-keeping on the guests' rooms while they were all in the session with the new professor. Todd, Cat reminded herself. And she was heading into the session. The door to Seth's area was right there. She could pop in and quickly ask if he was coming to lunch. She reached for the handle, and Deek came out of the den. "Oh, hi."

He looked at her, then back at the den door. "You did say it was okay for us to use that room, right?"

"Of course, you just startled me. How's the writing going?" She dropped her hand and fell in step with Deek, who had been on his way to the living room.

"Triple dog amazing. I can't believe how comfortable it is having a designated writing space. I just moved into my own apartment. It's over the bookstore. Anyway, it's great, but there's only three rooms, the bathroom, the bedroom, and the rest. I've set my desk up on the kitchen table, but my mom always moves the papers to one side when she comes to refill my fridge." Deek held up his hands. "I know, first world problems. And I love my mom taking care of me like that, but I'm thinking of buying a small desk to put in the dining area. The apartment came furnished but having a desk in there would make all the difference."

"Sometimes it's not where you write, it's the time and energy you put into your writing sessions. Some of my author friends write on a laptop and can write anywhere. Me, unless we're doing sprints, I write in my office on my laptop. I get what you're saying." Cat pulled out her phone. "I'm going to add that discussion to tomorrow's ask the author session. I think it's a good one, especially when you think about how you can take the 'retreat' and implement some of the processes at home."

"What a great idea. The three of us from South Cove, we already have a critique group that meets weekly. Maybe we should have a writing sprint night as well." Deek chatted on about his idea as they moved into the living room. The rest of the group was already there.

Cat interrupted Deek and asked him to find a seat. Then she went to the lectern to introduce their session lecturer. "Sorry that Deek and I were late; we were just talking about some ideas on how to bring the retreat home with you. He's got some amazing proposals for our South Cove guests. Tomorrow we'll be talking about it in our sessions, so think about it tonight and bring your ideas too. Today, we're excited to introduce our newest member to the Warm Springs Writers' Retreat experts, Professor Todd Lancaster from Covington College. I've asked the professor to talk about word origins and word choices in your writing. So I'll turn it over to Professor Lancaster."

Cat sat in the last available chair where she'd left her notebook earlier when she'd set up the room. Having something to write in gave her the chance to make notes if she wanted or to wander off and plan either the rest of the week or the next scene in her novel, depending on how boring the lecturer became. As a bonus, she always looked like a good, attentive student. It was a trick she'd learned to pull off during high school and it had never failed her yet.

After the professor had ended, the group gathered in the living room, talking about lunch plans. They were going to the Diner again. It was a popular place with visiting writers. The food was good and cheap. Stephen came over to Cat and pulled her aside from the group. "What's going on?" she asked.

He shuffled his feet and kept an eye on the rest of the group. "I don't want to miss them leaving for lunch. Having people around me this week, well, it's been a blessing. I appreciate you allowing me to continue with the retreat, even though, well, what happened."

"Stephen, you paid the fee. You belong here. But if you ever feel like it's too much, just let me know and I'll give you a credit for another week. You don't have to be here." Cat looked at the man standing in front of her. It was clear he wasn't sleeping well and his eyes looked a little dull, like he'd been hit with a train and didn't know where it had come from.

"No, I need to be here." He signed and held up a hand to Deek, letting him know he'd be ready in a few minutes. "They're kind and it helps me not think about how mad I am at Harriet. We could have been the perfect couple. Like you and your ex-husband. There was no reason I couldn't have worked at Covington, except for Harriet not wanting me there. She made our last few years hell. And as much as I hate her for that, I loved her still."

Cat watched as he walked over to Deek and the two men left the living room. Stephen was holding on by a thread, but she thought he was right about one thing. The friendship of the other writers was what was getting him through the day. Cat just wondered how he'd replace them starting Sunday when three of the four left for their normal lives.

Cat arranged the chairs back into a circle for their writing sprint time tonight and then headed to the kitchen. She felt bad for Stephen, but all she could do was keep the retreat happening like normal. That way, he'd have something to keep his mind off losing his wife.

Seth straightened in his chair as soon as she walked in the door. His voice was kind but wary. "Cat, what's wrong?"

She sank into her regular chair and sighed. "Nothing, really. I'm just sad for Stephen. He's trying so hard for life to just be normal and it's never going to be that way again. He misses Harriet."

Seth reached out and squeezed her hand. "You can't help everyone. Sometimes people have to go through hard things."

"I know. But for right now, Stephen's one of ours. And I'm going to make sure his time here is what he needs. I can't make him happy, but I can give him a strong retreat to distract him." She shook away any of the residual angst she'd brought in from the living room and the discussion with Stephen. "So, after that downer, how are you? I haven't seen you much this week."

"Sorry about yesterday. Phillip was in town, recruiting. I told him I was done, just like I'd said over the phone and in an email. I guess he needed to hear it in person."

"He'll probably come back," Cat said. This was her worst fear, that Seth wouldn't be able to say no to the military contract work since they would always need someone with his skill set.

"He might, but I know what I want. I want to be here with the two of you and working on this crazy house. Every time I think I'm close to being done, I find another disaster brewing. It's clear we're going to need a roof sooner than later. There is some water damage in the attic on the west side." He took a plate from Shauna with fried chicken and gravy-covered mashed potatoes. There was a large bowl of salad sitting on the table. "Thanks, Shauna, but it's not Sunday, is it?"

"It's not, but Pete called to say he'd be over for lunch, and I couldn't resist. He loves my fried chicken." Shauna set plates in front of Cat and then on the table for what appeared to be a spot set for Uncle Pete. She went back to fill one more plate. "He better show up soon. I told him I wasn't going to keep his plate warming. It will ruin the crust on the chicken."

"A new roof?" Cat turned the subject back to Seth's bombshell. "How much is that going to be."

"Around ten thousand. It's a big roof and we need to do all of it. I'll get some bids next week. Are you going to be able to float it? Or do

I need to wait until you talk to the bank. If you need a loan, I've got enough..."

The door opened and Uncle Pete came in. He stripped off his coat and started talking about the weather. "It's colder than it was supposed to be this week. I can't understand why they send those guys to college to learn how to predict the weather when they always get it wrong. I would think they should just have a pair of dice that has snow, rain, sun, and completely iced over as the four choices. That should cover it. They could just roll the dice before every broadcast."

He sat down and picked up his fork. Looking around the table, he sighed and set down his fork. "Okay, tell me what's going on. You three look like I stepped on your favorite kitten's tail."

"Seth was just telling us that the house needs a roof." Cat waved her fork at her uncle. "Go ahead and eat. I'm going to be over here having a pity party about the money pit I inherited. Michael's probably laughing from his grave. I bet he knew what a shambles the place was in."

This time, Uncle Pete reached over to squeeze her hand. "You love this house and you know it. If you need a loan, just let me know."

"That's what I told her." Seth nodded to Pete. "Good to see you. Shauna said you have news for us."

"Maybe not good news. Let's eat first and then we can talk." Uncle Pete dug into his meal, letting the sentence hang in the air.

8

Cat stared at her uncle. "You can't seriously think we're going to sit and eat after an announcement like that. Spill the beans."

"Look, Cat, I'm starving. I ate out of the vending machine last night since I was stuck at the station." He took a bite of the mashed potatoes. "Shauna, you've outdone yourself for a Tuesday lunch."

"High praise," Shauna said and her cheeks pinked. "Of course, you just told us you were starving, so maybe not such a high bar?"

"Not what I meant at all." Uncle Pete shook his head. "I'm saying all the wrong things to the women in my life lately."

"Uh, oh. Did something happen with Shirley?" Cat asked. Shirley had been one of the retreat guests and she and Uncle Pete had started a long-distance relationship right afterwards. Shirley lived in Alaska and used to be in law enforcement. Cat kept thinking that her uncle was going to announce soon that Shirley was moving to Colorado, but apparently, they weren't at that stage yet.

"I mentioned I hired Penelope and some of the ways she's made my life so much better. On the job, I meant. Shirley took it the wrong way." Uncle Pete set down the drumstick he'd just taken a bite out of. "I didn't mean she was making all my life better, just work."

"I've met Penelope and I'm not sure that's her goal." Cat didn't meet her uncle's glare although she could feel it. "Anyway, Shirley loves and trusts you. You just need to make sure your new employee realizes that's all she is. An employee."

"You're right. Penelope mentioned going to dinner a few days ago, but I blew it off as just wanting company. Maybe I haven't been clear with her. I'll fix it." He picked up the chicken again. "I don't suppose one of you wants to call Shirley and let her know I'm taking care of the issue?"

"Not on your life," Cat said but Shauna just laughed.

Seth held up his hands. "It's definitely not a dude thing. You need to fix this."

"Besides, Shirley scares Seth." Cat turned to smile at him. "Right?"

"She used to be in law enforcement. In Alaska. Of course, she scares me. If you thought about those two things, she'd scare you too." Seth didn't look up, he just kept eating.

"She's not that bad," Uncle Pete grumbled. "Okay, I'll handle what I broke with Shirley on my own. Thanks for the backup, guys."

"We didn't cause the problem," Shauna reminded him. "Since you don't have a leg to stand on with that discussion, do you want to tell us the bad news?"

He set his fork down, eyeing the still half-filled plate. "I just wanted to let you know that your 'guest,' Stephen, is being looked at hard for the murder."

"I thought you said he had to have been talking to Deek during the time of the murder? What's your theory, that he hired someone?" Cat leaned forward, trying to watch her uncle's response to her questions.

"The coroner came back with a time of death closer to midnight than nine which was in the original report. I guess the first guy there was a trainee who was sent out first because of how early it was. The coroner had told him just to bring back the body after doing his tests. He didn't know what he was talking about." Uncle Pete pulled up his phone and read off the text. "I work with idiots."

"The coroner sent that to you?" Cat tried to keep herself from laughing, but the grin was too hard to hide.

"He did. Then he called and explained the problem and gave me the real time of death. I don't think Harry's going to let a trainee take another call soon, even if it is at five in the morning. He said he had to redo all the paperwork. And there's one thing Harry doesn't like doing, it's paperwork." Uncle Pete set down his phone and resumed eating.

"So your working theory now is Stephen came home, killed his wife, dressed her in a zombie costume and then stuffed it in my barn. Right after he spent over a grand on attending a writers' retreat on the same property. Do you think he didn't realize the body would be found?" Cat didn't like that Stephen was the prime suspect or that he'd done it in cold blood. "I don't buy it."

"The other most likely motivation is that you got in a fight with Harriet and killed her in a rage over the fact she was working on canceling Covington's contract with you." Uncle Pete met her gaze and held it. "Do you want me to focus on that theory instead?"

"I didn't kill Harriet. Shauna and I had just talked about how we could get by without Covington's support. Except for the library, and we even found a way to get around that." Cat looked to Shauna for backup. "Right?"

"We don't need Covington's support. It's nice of course, and with needing the new roof, it would help sell the retreat, but we could make do without their support," Shauna said.

"Well, that's almost what you said when I told you I was worried about the upcoming hearing." Cat took another bite of the mashed potatoes. "Anyway, with or without needing a new roof, the retreat will go on even if Covington pulls its support. So I have no motive."

"Except Harriet Barring told several people last week that she thought you were sleeping with her husband and she was going to confront you at the party," Uncle Pete countered.

Cat almost choked on the potatoes. "One, I wasn't sleeping with Stephen. He's not my type. And, if you follow Aspen Hills gossip, it's supposed to be Dante I have a thing for and poor Seth." Cat tapped the fork on her plate. "I'm not sleeping with Dante, so neither one of those rumors are true."

"Well, that's nice to know," Seth mumbled.

Cat turned toward him. "You know the rumors aren't true, right?"

"Yes, Cat, I trust you. I know I messed up our relationship when I went out of country with the contract, and I know we're not talking about that, but I never worried about you cheating on me. Even after I pushed back the wedding date." Seth turned to Pete. "You can't believe what Harriet said, do you?"

Uncle Pete shook his head. "I don't. I know people just like to talk. But I wanted you to hear it from me, rather than on the street. I hate to have you punch someone because they made you mad."

"Seth wouldn't punch anyone," Cat protested.

Uncle Pete pushed his plate away and stood. "Actually, Catherine, I was talking about you. You have a bit of a temper."

After lunch was over and Uncle Pete had left, Seth pulled her aside out of the kitchen. "Cat, I believe you. I know we were in a bad spot for a few months there, but we were still a couple, and we still are. You understand, right?"

Cat nodded. "I know I didn't cheat, and I expect the same from you. Even now until we call it quits."

"Good. I thought I saw your wheels turning after your uncle left." Seth leaned back against the wall.

"Actually, you did. But not about us. I was thinking about how Harriet thought Stephen was cheating on her. Maybe it's the guilty calling out the innocent." Cat tapped her finger on her lips.

"What are you talking about?" Seth asked as he turned to look at her. "You think Harriet might have been having an affair and thought Stephen was too?"

"Sometimes people who are doing something wrong see themselves in other's actions." Cat heard a noise in the hallway and looked up to see Stephen on the stairs, watching them. From the look on his face, he must have heard what they were saying. "Stephen, I didn't expect you back this early."

"I left my writing notebook in my room. The group is writing at the library this afternoon and I needed my character sketches." He stepped backward to the main floor, then stepped toward them. "You think Harriet was cheating on me? I can't believe she'd do that. She was a pain, but we loved each other. For better or worse, you know, like the marriage vows."

"It's none of our business, but we were talking to Cat's uncle, the police chief, about who had motive to kill your wife." Seth stepped between Cat and Stephen, his pose protective, but relaxed. "The idea was thrown around."

"Well, you can tell him that even though Harriet and I fought a lot, we were both committed to our marriage vows. I was going to take her to Jamaica for our anniversary in January. She loved the beach. She was always working, but when she was on the beach, Harriet would actually relax. I loved seeing her that way." He wiped his eyes.

"Stephen, I'm so sorry. I know how devastated I'd be if I lost Cat." Seth put a hand on Stephen's arm.

He nodded, then turned back to the stairs. "Anyway, they're waiting on me in the lobby. I need to hurry."

Cat and Seth watched him sprint up the stairs. When she heard the guest room door close, she turned to Seth. "He's pretty certain she wasn't cheating."

"If she was, it's going to destroy him even more than he is now." Seth nodded to the door leading to his quarters. "Want to go see Sam? He's missing you. And we can talk about this more."

Cat nodded and followed Seth into the west wing. At least there, no one could overhear their conversation. And she felt like she needed some time away from the retreat and the murder. If Stephen didn't kill his wife, and she didn't think he had, then Uncle Pete had to look at the next likely suspect. Her.

She shivered as she entered the sun-filled living room. Even though she knew she hadn't killed Harriet, maybe the professor would get the last laugh and Cat would have to prove her innocence.

~

EVERYONE HAD SHOWN up for Tuesday's writing sprints session. The room was buzzing with excitement as Cat came into the room. Many of the writers were at the board, talking about their goals. Deek saw her and walked over to point at his numbers. "I was pretty sure I knew how much I could write in a sitting but doing the sprints at night has already upped my count. Do you think I'll still be writing this much at the end of the week?"

"You should be. Practicing writing in sections gives you the confidence to keep going. And once you hit your daily goal, you have the power to say you're done or if you're going to push out one more sprint. Words add up fast. That's one of the lessons you need to take home from the retreat. You may not hit your goal today, but if you write consistently, you'll be writing 'the end' before you know it."

Pixie had joined them near the front of the room. "What about edits? How do you divide that up? Or does this method work for editing?"

"I think the process works as well for edits. I set a daily goal of chapters. That way, I know what I need to get done to hit the deadline my editor gives me. If it's a project that hasn't sold—yet," Cat added with a smile, "you can set your own deadline and work backwards from that. That's one of the techniques we'll discuss tomorrow at the session with me."

"This is really good stuff." Pixie elbowed Deek. "And to think, I had to talk you into attending this, Mr. Big Shot with an agent looking at his manuscript."

"That's exciting. When did you send it?" Cat turned back to Deek who was blushing pink to match his dyed corn rows.

"Last week. I didn't want to say anything, but Pixie knew I'd been shopping the manuscript. My boss, Jill, gave me some names of authors to talk to and some of them gave me referrals to their agents." He shot a glance at Pixie who was grinning at him.

"Tell her how many requests for full reads you got." Pixie poked him. "I bet she says it's good too."

"Four out of six agents asked for a full. One wanted an exclusive, but I told her I'd already sent it out to another agent but would be glad to let her look too." Deek wiped his hand over his face. "That was one of the hardest emails I've ever sent. Then she responded right back saying, I figured. She did ask for the full though."

"You may have your choice of agents then. You'll need to talk to them all and see who meshes well with your personality. It's one of the most important relationships you'll have, so you need to trust that person." Cat glanced at the clock. "But it's already seven so we better get writing. How is everyone? Has everyone looked at their word count goal for the week? You can change it at any time. Up or down. No judgments. But the one with the most words will get bragging rights and a Warm Springs Writers' Retreat journal presented Saturday night. So make sure you update the board before we head to dinner Saturday."

"I'm sure that journal's mine then," Cari said from her chair where she already had her laptop open. "I'm going to kick butt and take names this week."

Pixie laughed as she moved back to a chair. "Well, I'm going to focus on words rather than sending out empty challenges. You know the turtle always beats the hare. And I'm nothing if not a turtle writer."

"Okay then, with that non-challenge set"— Cat glanced around the room— "is everyone ready for the first sprint of the night?"

"I am." Stephen raised his hand. "I'm not used to having all this free time to write. I'm usually in front of a class in Denver right now. I feel like I'm on vacation."

Cat thought it an odd thing to say since his wife had just been killed, but she let it go. Deek, on the other hand, gave Stephen an incredulous look. "Man, sometimes you can be so insensitive. Maybe you're not realizing you're probably in the grief process right now."

Stephen's face turned beet red. "You're right. I'm not sure why I even said that. I'm sorry if I'm sounding like a complete jerk."

"Everyone grieves differently." Cari reached over from her spot on the couch. "I'm sure you're still in shock. Just remember, we're here if you need us."

The group all agreed, with nods and a few "yes, we are" words of support called out. Cat held up the timer. "Okay, now are we ready to write?"

"You know I am," Stephen said looking around the room. "And I appreciate being able to be here with you all this week. You're making my transition less painful."

"Okay, I'm starting the clock now. We'll chat more in thirty minutes." Cat started the timer and then before starting her own writing, she looked around the room. Maybe having Stephen here wasn't the best idea, but at least this way, she could keep an eye on him. She wasn't completely sold on the "I loved my wife too much to kill her" routine, but on the other hand, he was handling her death way too easy. At least in her mind. If something had happened to Seth when he was gone, Cat would have been devastated. She wondered if that knowledge was the thing keeping her from moving forward again with Seth.

Either way, this wasn't her time to think about her relationship. She needed words. Good words or bad words, she needed to fill the page. As she'd agreed earlier, she set her thoughts about Seth aside and fell into Tori's prep for the first home game as a junior varsity cheerleader.

When the bell went off, everyone finished the sentence they were writing. Then she called out for word count, writing the numbers on the flip chart next to her. It was impressive how many words six people could get in thirty minutes. She pointed to the total number for that session. "Just think, if you scheduled six thirty-minute sessions for your week, you could be at this level or even more on your word counts. Sometimes it's just the idea of actually keeping track that's the magic."

"What if all the words are crap and we have to throw them out in edits?" Pixie asked as she stood and stretched.

"Then like Thomas Edison, you know one more way not to invent the light bulb. I'm a discovery writer so I have to think things out on the paper. I only know what's going to happen after I write it. Or at least the specifics of what's going to happen. Sometimes Tori, my main character, opens her mouth and I'm shocked at what she says.

Which is a good thing." Cat stood and stretched. "Ten-minute break. If you're doing a second round, get your snacks, bathroom breaks, and smokes in before seven forty. Or be really quiet when you come back into the room."

"Man, you really need to give yourself a break." Dalton patted Stephen on the back as they left the room. "Somethings happen for a reason."

Cat watched as the group headed out of the living room and toward the dining room where Shauna would have just dropped off the last bunch of snacks for the evening. Maybe having Stephen here was a good reminder of what was important in life.

Even for her.

9

The next morning, Cat woke early and headed upstairs to prepare for her session. She had a regular spiel, but she liked to add things based on each retreat's writers. Questions that had come up or she thought might, as well as questions around the specific type of books the group was writing. For this one, she assumed she'd be asked about the different publishers who bought paranormal books, the current state of the market for the subgenre, and the question that at least one person in every group asked, should I self-publish. She got out her folder and reviewed the notes she'd already made, then she added a few additional questions she thought she might be asked and went looking for the details for the answers.

Of course, the standard warning for all groups had been *your mileage may vary*. Each writer went about getting published in their own individual way. Writers who liked outside direction enjoyed having a publisher to set deadlines and give them support. Writers who were more internally motivated did better with self-publishing than others. If you never finished a book, it didn't matter how good the writing was. She also liked to repeat a piece of advice she'd heard from a lot of successful authors. Write three books, then try to get published. Writing a book was fun. Finishing it, that was a whole different story. A lot of would-be authors got four or five chapters in and got bored with the book. They'd blame the book idea or the genre and start another story. Finishing a book was harder than it seemed, and she wanted retreat guests to face that dragon sooner than later.

Cat finished her additions and realized she was out of coffee. Before going downstairs, she opened her manuscript and read what she'd written last night over the three sprint sessions. She tweaked a few words here and there, then picked up on the trail she'd built last night. Tori's first football game as a cheerleader had been a disaster. Someone in the coven had cast a spell to turn one of the girls from the squad green during the game.

Tori was on the hunt to see who in the coven was having a bad hair day now. The lesson of negative karma hadn't seemed to take with at least one of her witch friends. Cat was writing the scene where Tori and her witch rival, Katrina, were talking in Katrina's dorm room. Even with a towel over her head, the other witch was still trying to deny that she'd been the one to cast the spell. But when Tori saw the strand of emerald green hair fall out of the carefully wrapped turban, she knew she'd found the spellcaster.

Now, what to do with the rule breaker? Or was her own bad hair day enough to cement the lesson of *do unto others*? Tori was torn but she finally let the natural consequences do the punishment. A knock on the door brought Cat out of the story.

Shauna came in with a tray. "More coffee and a cinnamon roll for you. I knew you were probably busy working on your session, so I thought I'd bring sustenance up for you."

"Session is as done as it's going to get. It's always kind of fluid. Not like Professor Lancaster's lecture. You can tell he has a real love for the subject of word origins. He's done a lot of research for that class." Cat saved the document and then turned around and took the carafe from the coffee table where Shauna had placed the tray. "I'm working on a scene I started last night with the word sprints. I might have to implement sprint times on non-retreat weeks. Maybe you can come in and pretend you're writing with me."

"I don't think it works that way, but I could probably edit and write the introductions to the recipes. I like making them little stories." She sat down on the coffee table and poured a cup of coffee into the extra mug Cat hadn't seen.

"Uh oh, you've got some news for me." Cat pulled the cinnamon roll closer and broke off a bite. "Let me get the sugar high going before you burst my bubble."

"It's not that bad, but it's interesting. At least I think so." She took a piece of paper out of her pocket and handed it to Cat. "I got this from the university. They wanted us to know that due to the death of Professor Barring, our hearing would be with the dean and a different professor who's still arguing that Covington shouldn't support the retreat."

"Not surprising. I mean, I'd love it if our opposition had only been Harriet, but you have to know that a lot of the professors are on the same wavelength. If it's not literary, it's not real writing." Cat scanned the letter. It said exactly what Shauna reported. She took in a deep breath when she found the part Shauna hadn't said. "You have got to be kidding me."

"Nope. Professor Todd Lancaster is the new torch bearer for cutting off our funds. I think that's surprising since you had such a good discussion with him about hiring him for the editing sessions we're planning next year." Shauna sipped her coffee. "Did you have a clue he was so against our retreat?"

"No and that's sad, since I really enjoyed his lecture and I still think retreat guests would get a lot out of him being part of the team." She glanced at her watch. "Maybe I have time to go talk to him. See what his issues are."

"Cat, you might just hold off and see how the hearing goes. If their side loses, you can just be the bigger man and still hire him." Shauna sipped her coffee.

"You're thinking the rest there, aren't you? If we lose, do we trust him to be part of our team here?" Cat ate more cinnamon roll. "I hate it when people aren't upfront with me. If he didn't think the retreat was worthwhile, why did he say yes to talking yesterday?"

Shauna set her coffee down. "Do you think he was scouting the retreat out for Harriet? Planning to give her information so she could have countered our arguments and make us look like we're hacks?"

"That's a possibility. Or you've been watching too many spy movies. Of course, it is Aspen Hills. Weird things happen here." Cat took the last bite of the roll. That must be a land and sea eating record as fast as she'd devoured it. Emotional eaters are us.

"Maybe you should take someone with you if you go to the college to talk to him." Shauna moved the carafe off the tray and set the empty plate and fork on the middle. She drained her cup and set that on the tray as well. "I'm not doing anything this afternoon. Or maybe Seth?"

"If I take Seth, he'll be all macho about it. I just want to have a talk with Lancaster. You can call Uncle Pete if I go over an hour. He'll probably not even be there. Finding a professor on campus without just going in during their office hours is harder than tracking down a stray dog."

"That's a pretty image." Shauna stood and picked up the tray. "I'll let you get back to writing. Do you want me to come and get you for your session?"

"No, I've got an alarm set." Cat held up her smartwatch. "But if they come looking for me, feel free."

"Okay then. Just let me know before you take off to talk to the professor. I have a bad feeling about this." Shauna left the office and shut the door.

Cat turned back to the computer and glanced at the screen. Was she walking into the line of fire like her uncle would say? Or was it less covert that that? Maybe Lancaster agreed to be part of Harriet's crusade and his visit with the retreat wasn't as suspicious as it looked. Either way, she needed to find out what was going on.

She put away the questions that Shauna's announcement had started rolling around in her head and went back to Tori and her predicament. She needed to set the stage for a bigger conflict with this other witch, and the problem had started when Tori let her walk away from this first issue. Or at least that was the plan right now. Cat would let Tori figure out the plot as she wrote the words. It was story magic and it worked every time.

Her watch started beeping and she reluctantly logged off her computer. The words were flowing and she hated to stop when that was happening. Unfortunately, days like this were few and far between. Especially in this book where they were starting a new journey for Tori.

She picked up her folder as well as her cup and the empty carafe. She closed the door and put a hand on the outside. "I'll be back soon, Tori. You just figure out what's going on and I'll take notes."

Cat hurried down the stairs and dropped the dishes off in the kitchen. Shauna wasn't there so she grabbed a bottle of water and a cookie and headed into the living room to set up.

Cat copied the questions she always got from retreat guests, leaving room for new questions. She put her notes in front of her as she got ready, then she ate the cookie while waiting for the guests to arrive. As she waited, she thought about Lancaster and his role in the hearing. Maybe it was all just a coincidence. Harriet's face floated in her mind. On the other hand, a woman was dead. Everything needed to be examined to make sure Harriet's killer was found. Even just an education dispute about what was important in literature. One that could affect her livelihood.

During the session, Stephen looked distracted. When they took a break, Cat tried to pull him aside, but he was on his phone and left the house to talk. When they started up again, Stephen hadn't returned.

Deek held up his phone. "Stephen got called away on this murder investigation so he says to go on without him. He said he'll try to meet us at the Diner for lunch at twelve thirty."

With that mini mystery solved, Cat continued the session. When they broke for lunch, Dalton came up to her after the rest had left. "Hey, Dalton, do you have a question?"

He looked around the room and stepped even closer. "You know how you said you wouldn't tell the college about my book?"

"I stand by that. They won't hear from me that you're slumming it with us by writing paranormal fiction." Cat ripped the flip chart page off and folded it. She'd go back up to her office and make adjustments to the class after lunch. Or maybe after lunch and the trip to the college.

"Actually, I have something else I feel like I need to say, but I think it will just cause hurt feelings. And honestly, I didn't know about it when the thing happened. Once I found out, I broke it off immediately." Dalton was talking really fast and Cat worried she might know where this was headed.

"Dalton, I'm not a lawyer or a priest. You don't have to tell me anything." Cat tucked the flipchart into her folder and moved the stand into a nearby closet. She put the pens in a mug Shauna had put into the room for her use.

"But what if I want to? I need to tell someone, it's killing me. And if I tell you, then if you think someone needs to know it, you can tell him." Dalton looked up at her with unbridled hope.

She sat down next to him. "Fine, what do you need to tell me? I'm just going to give you fair warning: if it's a crime, I'm telling my uncle. Since he is the chief of police."

"Mmmmmhh, I hadn't thought about that." He rubbed his head. "Nope, I still think someone needs to know and I trust you."

"You just met me a few days ago," Cat reminded him.

"Yeah, but you're solid. I can tell that from you. And Deek says your aura is bright green, the sign of a kind and loving heart. I guess that's why I trust you." He looked around the room again. "I need to make sure no one hears us. I can't put this on someone accidentally."

"Okay, Dalton, spill. I've got things I need to do."

He adjusted his shirt, then he looked Cat straight in her eyes. "I slept with Stephen's wife, Harriet. I had Intro to Poetry last year and she wanted to help me with my poems. So we started meeting at night at her house, and then it happened. When I found out that she was married, I broke it off. Well, after class ended. I didn't need her to blackball me to the English department just because I didn't want to sleep with a married woman. That's a bad thing to say, right? Maybe she wouldn't have been vindictive, but I didn't want to take a chance. I'm here on scholarship. What if she told them I was the aggressor?"

Cat sat back, floored. She'd thought that maybe Harriet had been having an affair, but she'd assumed it had been with a fellow Covington professor. And that was why she didn't want Stephen to get a job at the college. That way, she'd have to come clean about the affair. But having sex with a student? Not even talking about the age difference, it was a power issue. That was one of the reasons she'd been so mad at Michael when they'd divorced. She had been concerned about what it would do to his reputation. Even though he'd already been labeled a flirt. They'd started dating when she was a teacher's assistant, but she was a graduate student, not an undergrad. And with his reputation, it hadn't been surprising. Even so, she hadn't been Michael's student, she was in a different department, and he hadn't been grading her term papers while they were in bed together. She realized Dalton was waiting for her to say something.

When she didn't respond, he sank onto the couch. "It's bad, isn't it? I knew I shouldn't be with her, but it was so exciting to have an older woman interested in me. Girls my age tend to see me as a joke."

"I'm sure that's not true, and if it is, maybe it's your behavior you need to work on." Cat leaned down, resting her hands on her legs. "Look, you're right. Having an affair with a married woman isn't a good thing to do. But you can't change the past. And I'm not sure telling Stephen is doing anything but making you feel better at this point."

"He'd be upset. He thought she was faithful. He told us that you and Seth were talking about Harriet. He said he told you that she wouldn't cheat. But she did. At least she did with me." Dalton leaned back in the couch. "I like Stephen. He's a good guy and I don't want to hurt him."

"Look, maybe telling him is important if you want to continue to be friends, but right now, it's going to gut him. Maybe you could wait a few months and if he's still in your life, you'll need to come clean then. If this friendship doesn't go past the retreat, you can just file it away as a life lesson learned." Cat paused a second, trying to wrap her head around the entire situation. "I think you need to tell my uncle though."

"The police chief? Won't he throw me in jail for killing Harriet?" Dalton's eyes widened and he sat up straighter, looking like he was ready to bolt out of there.

"Did you?"

Dalton blinked. "Did I what?"

"Did you kill Harriet?" She waited a beat while the question seeped into Dalton's brain.

He shook his head. "I swear, I didn't hurt her. I've been avoiding her since I cut it off. You should have seen the dagger eyes she was sending me the night of the party. It was scary."

"Then there's nothing to worry about. Uncle Pete needs to know if Harriet had a pattern of hooking up with students. Maybe one of them is the killer or one of the people who care about the student. Anyone could be the killer, it's just a matter of motive and accessibility. You need to make sure Uncle Pete knows that you didn't have motive, and hopefully, that you were with someone when she was killed."

"I was here, right?" He frowned then tapped the table. "No, the party was on Saturday night. Harriet and Stephen had this big fight. She was making me uncomfortable with the stares so I left with one of the local writing chicks and hit the Upper Classman for a drink. You know that new bar that's decorated like a cool frat house? We were there until two, I left with a girl in one of my classes, and she was still in my room the next morning. That's an alibi, right?"

Cat saw he was truly happy he'd cleared himself of the murder. Now, he just had to tell the same story to Uncle Pete and have the girl confirm it. "Sounds like one to me. Do you want me to call my uncle?"

"I'll just stop by the police station on the way to lunch. I should be able to get in and out of there in no time. Especially since all I know is I slept with Harriet almost two years ago." He stood and moved to leave. "Thanks for talking to me about this. I know it's a little out of the range for subjects you thought you might be counseling writers on, but you're really good at it."

Cat watched Dalton leave. She was wiped out and wasn't going to be getting any more writing done today.

As she made her way upstairs to put away her file, she wondered: if Harriet wasn't sleeping with Dalton now, was she sleeping with anyone? She still needed to go talk to Professor Lancaster. Maybe he knew something about who Harriet hung around with. Her uncle couldn't blame her if information about Harriet had just dropped into her lap, could he?

10

By the time Cat arrived at the English department, the hallway of offices on the third floor for the non-tenured professors appeared deserted. She found Lancaster's office with a note about open office hours being limited to an hour before and after each class he taught. Looking at his posted schedule, she'd have to come around five pm or wait until eight pm on Monday, Tuesday or Friday. Since she had a retreat in session, none of those days would work this week.

Maybe Shauna was right. The hearing was late next week. Talking to Lancaster might just make her mad. If he was against the retreat getting Covington money, she would just find another professor to do the second, editing-focused session. She had time before they changed up the program anyway.

She took the stairs back out of the building, but when she entered the staircase, she heard voices below her. She slowed her pace when she heard someone mention Harriet Barring's name. Pausing mid floor, she tried to hear more of the conversation.

"Can you believe that guy got all of Harriet's classes? He'll be on track for tenure starting next semester, mark my words."

Another voice added, "He's such a suck up to the Dean. But I guess you have to be if you're even going to be considered for promotions around here. Harriet wasn't a supporter of other female professors, but at least she was one of the few females who actually achieved tenure here at Covington. Ten to one the next person to get tenure will be male. I'm not sure why I stay, except I'd have to start all over at a new university. I'm hoping this paper will get me some offers from other colleges. Then I can tell them what they can do with their backwoods college."

The door opened and the speakers must have left through the second-floor hallway. From Cat's experience, the new to Covington professors and the teachers' assistants were housed on that floor. She hurried out of the building, wondering if Harriet's death had anything to do with her job. It didn't sound like she made waves, well, except for her rally against Cat's retreat. She'd already achieved tenure, so there was no reason to kill her to get her out of the pool. Having her tenure spot would only help the next person in line. Cat wondered who that might be. Just because Lancaster had taken her classes didn't mean he was up for the next tenure position. And his office location seemed to say he considered a tenure track hopefull. But she'd put a bug in her uncle's ear for him to check it out, just in case.

She hurried home, hoping to carve out more time with the manuscript. The problem with writing during retreat weeks was she was constantly being interrupted. And once her flow had been cut off, sometimes she was too tired to jump back into the story line.

Sometimes she thought writing was like hooking a hose up to a part of your body and something pumped the story in while you transcribed it onto the page. She'd spent a few summers transcribing reports for her uncle from audio recordings. She'd listened to the words, wrote down what she'd thought it said, then listened again to make sure. Writing at times felt like that, transcribing the story from another source. Some people called it the muse. For some, it was the passing down of story from one generation to the next. And others just called it making crap up.

She didn't know where the inspiration came from, she just loved polishing the story she'd created into something that she was proud of. And that took time and lots of butt in chair time.

SHAUNA CAME UPSTAIRS to pull her out of the zone to eat dinner. Cat's eyes were burning from writing so much, but she was proud of what she'd done. If she didn't get more words during the sprints tonight, she'd edit what she wrote this afternoon. Then she'd crash until tomorrow when she'd do it all again.

"You looked drained. Do you want me to run the sprint group tonight?" Shauna offered as they made their way downstairs to the kitchen.

"I think I can do it. At least I'll start, you might have to finish, or I could ask Deek to run the group." Cat rolled her shoulders as they walked. "Is Seth joining us?"

"Seth and your uncle are already in the kitchen. He hasn't said outright, but I think he's having trouble with his new hire. She seems to be very particular about how she runs her station."

Cat turned her head and saw Shauna grinning. "Her station?"

"Yeah, he asked me if I'd consider taking on the admin duties of the police station for him." Shauna paused just outside the door to the kitchen.

"What did you say?"

"That he couldn't afford me." Shauna pushed the door open. The men stopped talking when they walked into the room. "Don't stop on our account. We love listening to baseball stats."

"Actually, we were talking football. It's the wrong season for baseball." Seth corrected her and then stood to get drinks out of the fridge for the women. "Drinks?"

"Please." Cat sat down at the table. "One thing I've learned about sports is no matter what the season, there's usually something to talk about. Like trades or contracts or even the trouble the players get in when they aren't working out."

"Well, no more sports talk tonight. I want to hear about the retreat." Uncle Pete took a roll from the middle of the table and buttered it. "How are your guests doing with the murder?"

"Honestly, they're here to write, not to talk about a murder," Cat said, but then she sighed. "Except some of them are. How do you know these things?"

"Cat, you had a murder in your barn. Why do you think they wouldn't be talking about it? I take it Stephen's been chatty?" He leaned back as Shauna set a bowl of beef stew in front of him. "Thank you, it looks and smells amazing."

"Of course, we love having you over for dinner. Even if you're here hiding from your new hire." Shauna smiled sweetly, then set a bowl in front of Seth.

"That's a story I want to hear," Cat teased as she waited for Shauna to finish. She'd asked long ago if she could help, but Shauna said it was easier for only one person to be moving around in the kitchen. Which meant Cat was clumsy. "Anyway, Stephen's convinced Harriet wasn't having an affair. And I just got told that he was wrong. She had at least one."

"Another professor I bet. That's why she insisted Stephen take the job teaching in Denver." Shauna broke open a roll as she talked.

"That might have been why she wanted Stephen in Denver, but this affair was a student. At least that's what he told me today." Cat waited for the implication of her words to hit the group.

"No. Dalton?" Shauna's eyes widened. "The guy can't be over twenty-five, maybe twenty-six."

"And this was a few years ago when he was an undergrad." Cat dipped a roll into the stew. "I know Michael had a rep for dating students, but besides, me, I don't think he ever did. Intentionally. And I wasn't his student when we started dating. Professors get annual lectures about the conflict of interest and the power dynamics. Dalton called it off right after he found out she was married. Well, after his class ended with her."

"How pragmatic of him." Uncle Pete focused on his meal. "Anyway, he's already stopped by the station and told me. I don't think if what he said pans out to be true that he's going to be high on my suspect list. It's unfortunate that relationships like this happen way too often at Covington. Even with the annual warning."

Cat saw the look he'd given her at the end of his statement. He'd never liked Michael, mostly because her uncle had thought the older man had taken advantage of Cat when she and Seth had been having problems. Seth had wanted her to apply to graduate schools near where he was stationed so they could start their life together. Cat had wanted to work at Covington since she'd visited the college in junior high.

She decided to leave the subject be. "So any new developments? Is Stephen still high on the suspect list?"

"You know I can't tell you that." Her uncle's gaze went back to his dinner. "Especially since you're still on the list."

"That's stupid," Shauna said, but Cat shook her head.

"Leave him alone, Shauna. He's doing his job. Harriet was very vocal about the retreat and how Covington shouldn't be sponsoring it. I know and you know that I didn't kill her, but now we have to find out who did." Cat was surprised to see her uncle glaring at her after she'd been so supportive of his investigation style. "What did I say wrong?"

"I'm finding out who killed Harriet, not you or Shauna or Seth or even your little writer group. Remember when they went up to the ghost town to try to clear someone's name? Your writer groups tend to think they're all living in a detective novel when they show up in Aspen Hills." Uncle Pete nodded to the stove. "Okay if I get seconds?"

"Of course. I can get it." Shauna started to stand but Uncle Pete waved her down.

"You do enough around here. I can refill a bowl." The conversation paused as he went to the stove.

When he returned, Seth spoke up. "You know, if there wasn't a murder investigation going on when the retreat guests showed up, they might just focus on their writing."

Cat snickered when Uncle Pete gave Seth the side-eye.

"Fine, I'll just send a letter out to the general public and ask that they refrain from killing anyone during retreat weeks." Uncle Pete closed his eyes and then sighed. "Sorry, folks, I'm a little worked up from today. Do you know that the woman has been blocking Shirley's calls? I got a text from her asking if I was sick because I was never at the office."

Cat grabbed a second roll, and this time she put butter on it. "It doesn't surprise me. I thought she was going to kick me out of your office when I came in to wait for you to get off the phone. She's a little controlling."

"She's done a great job at getting the station under control, but I'm going to chat with her first thing in the morning about boundaries. If I set them now, maybe she'll work out. Otherwise, I'll be looking for a new administrator for the station."

"Wow, I'm glad I'm not in your shoes. I get in enough trouble around here with these two. And I know my boundaries." Seth stood and refilled his bowl.

Cat noticed he left the cane at the table and his limp was less pronounced today. She thought about saying something, but it might just be a good day. He'd been shot, but not the why's behind the mission, saying it had been classified. Cat didn't know if the army sent contractors into classified situations.

He was back home. He was safe. And he was alive. That's all she cared about. She turned to her uncle. After hearing the rumors in the stairwell, she was curious.

"Uncle Pete? Have you heard anything about a new tenure position coming up? They should be hiring for Harriet's spot, right?" Cat didn't know how much of the internal processes of Covington her uncle had any insight on. He met with the president of the college weekly, so she assumed at least Harriet's death had been discussed.

"I'll ask John tomorrow when we meet for breakfast. He's assured me that the families are claiming no interest or involvement in the murder. So if it was one of the specials, the powers that be weren't part of it." His phone buzzed and he responded to the text. "I've got to go. Someone just broke into the building that houses the English department."

"Just to be clear, I was there today. I went to see if Professor

Lancaster was really against Covington sponsoring the retreat. So you'll find my fingerprints may be in the lobby, the elevator, the third floor, and the stairwell down to the exit." Cat recited every place she'd been when she'd stopped by that day. Just in case. "Oh, and the women's restroom on the first floor."

"You always make my job interesting, Cat. Thank goodness there's only one niece in our family to mess up my life." He finished the last of the stew. "Thank you so much for dinner, Shauna. It was kind of you."

"You sounded like you were having a bad day when you called earlier." Shauna picked up his bowl. "Do you want some in a to go container for lunch?"

Uncle Pete shook his head. "I'd love some, but I'm not sure when I'll be home. I hate to have it go bad if it has to be in my car for a few hours."

"If you give me a second, I'll get it packed in a cooler, that way you have lunch tomorrow if your day's busy." Shauna hurried to pack up some of the stew.

He stood and took his bowl and silverware to the sink. "You always make this easy. Accepting help, I mean. I appreciate your concern. Especially now when I see the way Penelope has tried to worm her way into my life. If love charms were real, I'd be in big trouble."

"Hey, how do you know spells aren't real," Cat asked.

Her uncle took the cooler from Shauna. "Because if they were, Penelope would already have used one and Shirley would be on the plane from Alaska trying to save me from the woman's charms."

"With that bit of storytelling, I'm going into the dining room to check on the treat supplies. These guys love their brownies. But they haven't even made a dent in the cookie supply I put out this morning." Shauna laughed as she walked toward the hallway.

Pete reached out to the counter and stuck a few cookies in his shirt pocket. "I'll help out with that problem."

After Shauna and Uncle Pete left, Cat cleaned off the table and put the dinner dishes in the dishwasher. When Seth carried over the empty roll basket, she took it from him. "You look like you're feeling good today."

"You're watching me?" Seth lifted his eyebrows. "Should I be blushing?"

"I'm making sure my contractor is getting healthy to finish my remodel. Are we still on track for January? I'd like to start announcing the new editing session soon." She turned and watched him return to the table, sitting down in the chair. He reached down and rubbed his leg.

"I'm getting stronger. The exercises that I got in therapy really help. I go back next week to check on my progress." He gathered the salt and pepper shaker and moved them closer to the side of the table. "I hate being useless."

"You're not useless. You did the airport pickup this month. And you've been painting, even though I think you might be pushing it too much." She sat down next to him. "Seth, I care about you. You need to take the healing slow."

"I'm fine." The stubborn line formed on his forehead. Cat knew she needed to back off. He didn't want to hear about his injury affecting what he could do.

"I know. Were you tempted when you were offered another mission?" Cat picked up the seasonings and put them over on the counter. Then she brought over a rag to wipe the table.

"Not at all. One, I'm not physically ready. And two, I'm not going out again. This mission, well, it scared me. I have never felt like I wasn't coming home before. This last time, I did. I won't risk it again. I won't risk us again. Even if the money's really, really good."

Cat finished wiping the table and went back to the sink. She wanted to believe him, but he'd said he wasn't going back before and then he did. Before she could respond, the door to the hallway opened and Shauna came back into the kitchen with several carafes.

"I definitely need to restock the coffee and hot water." Shauna looked at Cat and Seth. "Did I interrupt something? Do you need me to leave?"

"No, I was just going back to let Sam out. He needs some exercise.

Since I can't run right now, it will have to be chasing the ball time."
He picked up his cane, and Cat saw him using it to leave the kitchen.

When he was gone, Shauna washed out the carafes. She turned to
Cat. "He doesn't fool me. He'd going to sit for a while and get off that
leg."

"Yeah, but he'll do it out on the deck and throw the ball to Sam
while he's resting. The man can't stay still for even a minute. Unless
he's watching football. And we've got him driving to Denver on
Sunday so he'll miss some of the games." Cat nodded to the doorway.
"Can I help with the dining room? If I sit here, I'm going to fall
asleep."

"You could just go up and relax." Shauna laughed when Cat
shook her head. "You and Seth are two of a pair. Neither one of you
knows how to just sit and relax. I think sending you to the beach for a
week would kill you. Or you'd find a local charity to work at while
you're there. Go ahead and clear off the dishes in the dining room.
When you get that done, we'll restock everything."

Cat took a tray out and while she was cleaning, she started
thinking about the next step in Tori's adventure. She wouldn't get a
lot of words tonight, and she'd probably only stay for one sprint, but
she thought she had a few more words in her before she needed to
shut her mind down.

11

On the schedule, Thursday was a free day for the writers. Shauna had given them a list of suggestions in their welcome baskets, but Cat liked to check in during their breakfast to make sure they had found the list and to see what everyone was planning.

She'd gotten up early and had already finished the chapter she'd started last night. The words flowed better for her in the morning. She knew some writers were night owls, but she was definitely a lark, someone who wrote early before the day weighed her down. Now, she was in the kitchen with her calendar, making sure she'd added the retreat business stuff onto her work calendar.

"I'd like to set up the west wing guest rooms with a different theme than the others. Maybe we can splurge and set each room up with a small writing desk, making it more writer focused? A bookshelf in every room?" Shauna was throwing out ideas.

"That's a lot of books. I know we still have some of Michael's that the library didn't take or already had, but writers don't want shelves full of economic studies." Cat tapped her pen on her planner. "Maybe we can look at the consignment and charity shops for books. People are always giving away their stashes. I can put a full Tori collection in each room with the free books my publisher sends me."

"And we can add my cookbooks too." Shauna pointed to the next free Saturday. "Want to take a trip into Denver on this day to scour shops? If we don't find what we need, we can do it again next month. I'd rather have too many books than not enough when the rooms are ready."

"Let's make it the weekend after. I need to have time for this deadline and the hearing. If I have an emotional day, you know it's going to affect my writing." Cat circled the day of the hearing on her calendar. "I'm not doing anything on this day. It's going to be draining enough without me trying to write."

"We'll look for furniture too." Shauna stood and dumped the rest of her coffee. "I'd like to have a refinishing project or two for the fall."

"I can't believe how much stuff you get done. I'm still trying to figure out how to fit the writing and the retreat into my life. I'm so drained by the end of the retreat, I'm sleeping ten hours a day for the next week."

"I do things that aren't people focused so I get a lot more recovery time during the actual retreat than you do." Shauna turned around from the window and focused on Cat. "You're the face of the retreat. And you're an introvert. So after a retreat, you need to shut down for a while."

"Maybe you should take over part of the upfront and personal time at the retreat." Cat looked at the clock. "If I'm going to catch everyone, I need to go now."

"Take me up on my offer next time you need someone take over the sprint time. I'm perfectly able to do that, and it would give you at least one night off during retreat week," Shauna reminded her.

"I will do that," Cat said as she headed out to the dining room. She counted heads and everyone was sitting at the table, enjoying one of Shauna's quiches. "Good morning, everyone. I'm sure you noticed that there isn't a planned session for today. Instead, I want you to take this time to either relax, work on your own, go sightseeing, or set up writer sprints throughout the day."

"There's a hot springs at the end of town. It's walkable from here and it has amazing views," Dalton suggested. "They've built a full-size pool as well as several hot tubs for your use. It's not too pricey and you feel amazing when you leave."

"I'd probably be asleep as soon as we got back." Cari rolled her shoulders. "But I'm game if we can do it after lunch. I'd like to get some words in this morning."

"I need to write some agent letters and work on the outline for book two in this series," Deek added. "I'd be totally down for an after-lunch outing."

The others nodded and added their morning plans to the mix. Cat broke open a muffin and ate it while they talked. She stood after the writers had come up with their plan for the day. "Okay, I'll be in the living room at seven if anyone's awake to do sprints."

"You should come to the hot springs with us," Pixie said. "I'd love to hear more about your start and what you think about the industry now."

"I think you should all go back to school and become doctors or lawyers and make tons of money," Cat teased. "I'm thinking the hot springs is a no, but I'll check in before you leave, just in case I change my mind."

A voice came from the doorway. "I think the hot springs is a definite yes, if I'm invited."

Cat turned to see Seth standing there, a can of paint and a bag in his hands. "If you want to go, I'll go."

"You should tell Shauna too," Pixie chimed in. "Then it's an official retreat road trip."

"I'll probably drive, so if anyone wants to ride in the bus there or back, you're welcome to join me," Seth offered. "I'll be out front at one."

"This sounds awesome." Deek leaned back in his chair. "My shoulders could use a good soak. Is there a legend about the hot springs?"

"You mean an old Indian legend about the hot springs having

healing powers or something like that?" Seth set his bags from the hardware store down and came in to get a glass of orange juice.

"Wow, really?" Deek was leaning forward now, his hands clasped together to hear the story.

"Not that I know of. What about you, Cat?" Seth leaned on the wall.

Cat laughed. "Seth's teasing me because when we were kids, there was a ghost story about the hot springs. So naturally, we broke in one night to see if the ghost of an old gold panner really showed up at midnight on the full moon."

"Did he?" Pixie was transfixed by the story.

She shook her head. "No, and my uncle was on duty that night. Since the story was so well known, on most full moon nights, someone would at least try to break in. We knew someone who worked at the hot springs and copied his key. But we got to swim for a while before my uncle saw the lights."

"Cat got grounded for a month. My mom only laughed and said she hoped the chief was going to put me in jail for my crime." Seth flashed a grin toward Cat. "But your uncle sat me down and explained the rules of dating the niece of someone in law enforcement. I think I was lucky not to be sent off to boarding school."

"You two are too cute." Pixie laughed as she peeled a banana. "Were you high school sweethearts too?"

Seth and Cat looked at each other and he spoke first. "Cat was my first and only love. She and I were meant to be. But a handsome professor swept her away and I had to come running to her rescue once the guy left her alone."

"I heard you divorced him for an affair with a co-ed." Stephen looked bored and a little red eyed.

Cat wondered if the attitude was from his situation or if he was hung over. She'd heard him and Deek leave last night after the sprints and the door entry code showed them coming back after midnight. Deek shot him a look.

Cat held up a hand to stop Seth from talking. "Michael and I did divorce and I got the house back through an inheritance when he died. I don't think why we divorced is relevant."

Stephen's face turned beet red. "But my wife's transgressions seem to be fodder for everyone's discussions."

"Dude, uncool," Deek shot back.

Stephen stood and wavered. "Sorry, I'm not in the mood for talking with anyone today. I'll be in my room."

After he left the dining room and they'd heard his footsteps on the stairs, Deek sighed. "Sorry about that. I think he drank too much last night at the bar. I went with him because I wanted to talk about what it was like as a professor, but all he wanted to do was drink. I should have left him there, but I didn't feel like he could make his way back. I did have a lovely discussion with the bartender. She's attending Covington on what she called the townie scholarship. She's in journalism."

"That would be Cassie Carrol and she's very nice. I think she's a junior now. Cat and I went to school with her uncle." Seth set his juice glass down. "I'm off to work. Especially if I'm playing hookie this afternoon at the hot springs. The car will be ready at one."

The guests started leaving and Deek stayed back to talk to Cat. "Sorry about that," he said.

"It wasn't your problem or your words." Cat cleared the table as they talked.

"No, but I saw your face when he said them. Stephen's hurting and it looks like he just moved into the anger side of grief. If he wants to go to the bar tonight, he's on his own."

"It's your retreat. You aren't responsible for anyone else here besides yourself. But if Stephen becomes a problem, I might have to deal with it." Cat picked up the last plate. "I don't want anything or anyone to ruin your retreat experience."

"Oh, he's not. I'm so far ahead of where I thought I'd be. I've started writing the second book, just in case, but I'm hoping I'll get a contract for the first one soon. I almost signed with someone a few months ago, but I found out that he was more of a vanity publisher. If I'm responsible for all the costs, I'd rather go the self-publishing route and get most of the money." Deek put two cookies on a napkin. "I'm sorry Stephen attacked you though. That wasn't fair."

"It kind of was. I was talking about Harriet with Seth in the hallway when Stephen caught us, so he wasn't wrong." Cat glanced around the dining room. It looked respectable, but she still needed to wash off the table.

As if she'd been called, Shauna showed up with a rag and a trash bag. "Oh, I didn't think anyone was still in here."

"We're just talking. The group is going to the hot springs this afternoon and has invited us to go. Seth's taking the van if you don't want to walk." Cat filled her friend in on the plans.

"It's supposed to be a nice day," Deek added. "You both have been so welcoming; it would be nice to get out and have a bit of a break."

Shauna washed off the table. "I don't think I've ever been to your hot springs. Cat and I used to spend afternoons at the beach together if she wasn't teaching. Lots of cute surfer dudes."

"Well, I didn't bring my surfboard, but I have my crazy colored California trunks." Deek smiled and Cat swore the birds started chirping outside.

"How can I refuse?" Shauna laughed as she went to change out the trash bag. "I'd be glad to come with you all."

Deek left the room and Cat caught Shauna's gaze. "He's pretty hot."

"He's also too young for me." Shauna tied up the trash bag and looked around the dining room. "We need more brownies again. I'd swear your group thinks they're made with a special ingredient."

"I think Pixie just likes chocolate." Cat followed her friend into the kitchen. They talked a while and Cat was just about to head upstairs to see if she could get another scene done when the door to the kitchen flew open.

Stephen came into the room, holding what looked like a planner. "I need to talk to your uncle. I think maybe I was wrong about Harriet."

"Wrong? About what?" Cat didn't move toward him but she

hoped he'd at least sobered up since their last encounter. "And what's in your hand?"

Stephen pointed to the book. "It's Harriet's calendar. I pulled it from her office on Saturday night when I got home. I thought maybe she was out with someone. And yes, I suspected she was having an affair before I heard you talking about it. I just didn't want to admit it."

"I don't understand. You pulled her planner why?" Cat reached out from where she was sitting and took the book from him. He sat next to her and pointed at it.

"Like I said, after I left the party, I walked home. And things just kept bothering me. Like how I couldn't reach her when I was on break from working. Or how she'd say she tried to call me, but the call hadn't gone through. Mountain passes and cell phones just don't work. It all sounded normal when she said it." He leaned back in his chair. "But something she'd said at the party had ticked me off. Like I was less of a person because I worked at the community college rather than Covington."

"So when you went home you went to her office and got her calendar?" Cat flipped through the pages. Harriet had blocked off several nights a week, and with the block, it had Stephen's work schedule. It didn't look suspicious if you weren't looking for it. Just a wife making sure she didn't make plans her working husband couldn't attend.

"No, when I got home, I went to talk to her. To ask her point blank if she was having an affair. She wasn't home. Even though she'd left the party hours before me. That's when I knew. I went to get her calendar. But by then, I was beat. I knew I was coming to the retreat, so I tucked it in my bag, thinking I'd have time to read it when I got here. And if she asked where it was, I'd just play dumb." He looked at Shauna. "Do you happen to have some coffee in here? I can go to the dining room if you want me to."

"No, I'll get you a cup. Cream or sugar?"

"Just black, thanks." He smiled then turned back to Cat. "Then I heard about Harriet and I'd forgotten about the calendar. After I made a fool of myself downstairs this morning—sorry, by the way—I remembered what I'd thought about Saturday night and dug out the planner. She had time blocked for almost every night I was out of town teaching. And there's a code by each block."

Cat looked at the week before Harriet's death. H2208 was written in one block and A3790 in the other. The third block only had Stephen's name and Denver written on the top of the block like the other two. "It could be word count and a project code. Didn't you say she was working on a special project?"

"She wouldn't talk to me about it. She was superstitious about her writing. I thought this might be word counts, but look at this week." Stephen took the cup from Shauna, nodding his thanks.

Cat turned the page. The numbers were the same, but sometimes, they were switched on different days. It couldn't be word counts unless she wrote exactly the same number of words as she'd goaled every day. Which was OCD, even for Cat. She flipped back some pages and noticed the coding had started in September. And was only on days that also had Stephen's class notation with the times. She picked up the phone and dialed. Uncle Pete picked up on the third ring. "Why are you answering the station line?"

"Because as of a few minutes ago, I am without an office administrator. What do you want, Cat? I'm a little busy here." Uncle Pete sounded stressed.

"I don't know. Did you want to see Harriet's calendar? Or are you too busy for that?" Cat smiled at Stephen who looked confused.

"Where did you find it? We've been looking for it since this thing started. I was beginning to think the woman only used a digital planner."

"Stephen had it." She saw the look of fear on his face and tried to calm him. "Shall I send him over or do you want to come here?"

"Send him down. I'm on phones until my relief officer arrives. She had to drop off her kid at daycare since Penelope cut the woman's hours last week." Uncle Pete swore under his breath. "The boards are lighting up. I've got to go."

And then she was talking to dead air. She set the phone down.

"Go to the station and take this to my uncle. Show him what you showed me. Do the numbers mean anything to you?"

He shook his head. "I thought maybe the last four of a phone number, but I went through her address book in the back and they're not listed as anyone's."

She handed him back the calendar. "Well, it means something. Thanks for letting me see it. Are you going to come to the hot springs later?"

"If your uncle doesn't throw me into jail for not telling him about having this, yes. I need to make my apologies to the group and Deek for being such a jerk this morning." He stood and headed to the back door. "No time like the present. Does this go around to the front?"

"Just turn left and follow the path," Shauna answered. Then she sat down next to Cat. "That was unexpected. I'm sorry I missed breakfast. Was he really that big of a jerk to you?"

"Yes. I was on the verge of telling him to leave until he got his head straight, but I think he might be on the right path now. You can't write when you're that emotional. And what you do write is usually crap. The muse likes a clear line to your thinking and alcohol tends to make that line fuzzy." Cat stood and stretched. "I'm going to see if the muse is hanging out in my office this morning. I think after I sit in the hot springs for a while, I'm not going to feel like writing tonight."

"I think Hemingway might have disagreed with you," Shauna called after her. "Looking forward to this afternoon."

As she walked upstairs to her office, Cat realized she was looking forward to a worry-free afternoon of fun too. She just hoped nothing would happen to cut that buzz.

12

Cat was surprised to find her uncle's Charger in front of the house when they arrived back from the hot springs. The writers were getting changed and ready for a night out. Cat had told them that she wasn't attending the nightly sprint, but that they were okay to write without her. Deek offered to run the session as she'd suspected he might. Stephen seemed lighter and Cat caught him smiling as the group chatted on the walk back. Only Seth and Shauna had taken the van back from the hot springs and it was already parked in the driveway. She told the writers to have a great dinner and headed into the kitchen to see what her uncle was up to.

The three of them were huddled around the table and looked up when she opened the door. She slipped into a chair and leaned back, her neck muscles loose from the magic of the hot water. She really needed to go there more often. Especially when she was on deadline. "Hey, guys, did I miss a meeting?"

"I just came to tell you that there's been a break in the Barring murder." He sipped his coffee, then opened the notebook. "According to my source, and I quote, Miss Latimer mentioned several times wanting to kill Harriet Barring to stop the hearing process."

The room was quiet and Cat let the words sink into her brain.

"Wait, someone said I told them I wanted to kill Harriet? Who exactly did I say this to? The only person I would say something like that to would be Shauna and she knows I'm just blowing off steam."

"See, that's the thing, Cat. You open your mouth when you shouldn't say anything. Then you're a sitting duck when something happens." Uncle Pete clicked his pen and held it over the notebook. "Tell me again, what happened on Saturday night?"

"The whole thing? Or where do you want me to start?" Cat felt her neck muscles tightening again. What a waste of a soak.

"From the first time you saw Harriet to the time you woke up the next morning." Uncle Pete must have seen the frustration on her face. "Cat, I need to clear you. Especially with this professor coming in and giving this damning statement. I don't know what you did to get on this guy's bad side, but you have him upset."

She went through the timeline as she remembered it, including her first sighting of Harriet. "Seth was with me and he can tell you that I didn't go over to accuse her of backstabbing me then drinking my wine."

"Because I told you to leave it alone," Seth reminded her. "Can you remember who was nearby that might have overheard us talking?"

"We were standing near the bar. Mostly everyone except Harriet, Stephen, and Tammy. They were on the other side of the room, talking." She shook her head. "No one stands out. I don't know who all heard me complain about Harriet being there. A lot of people heard them fighting though. They had several incidences of raised voices."

Uncle Pete sighed and closed his notebook. "Your story hasn't changed at all since the last time we talked. I know you didn't kill Harriet. I just don't know what this Professor Lancaster has against you."

Cat and Shauna's gaze met. "You're kidding, right? Todd Lancaster filed the statement?"

Uncle Pete nodded. "Why is that significant? I can tell by that look it is a problem."

"He's the professor we asked to come talk to the writers this session. When I found out that Covington sent us a poet, I wanted to make sure he got something from the programming, but apparently he's secretly writing a novel. So no outing him. Anyway, Todd was really good. I thought he might do a talk for us when we start taking a second retreat at the first of the year."

"You're telling me he had a reason to *not* tell me about what he heard. You're not helping your case here. Did you notice any negativity when he talked to the writers? Any hint of a mental illness perhaps that would cause him to do something so much out of his character? A need to jeopardize his career so he could torch yours?" Uncle Pete looked at Shauna, then Cat.

"We found out that he replaced Harriet on the panel that's against Covington sponsoring the retreat. That's why I was at the campus yesterday and why I was in the English building specifically. I wanted to talk to him. That reminds me, what was taken from Harriet's office?"

"I never said anything was taken." Uncle Pete narrowed his eyes but then he turned pages in the notebook. "Her assistant said there was some candy missing from the top drawer, but she didn't know if Harriet finished it off on Saturday since the janitorial staff comes seven days a week and would have dumped her trash bin. That was her last day at in the office until Monday. And by then she knew Harriet was dead, so she consulted the college attorneys, who basically told her to keep going to work until they told her not to. I'm thinking they might have been looking for something that wasn't there."

"From the gossip I heard in the stairwell, Lancaster is not only taking over Harriet's crusade against the retreat, he's also taking over her classes." Cat tapped her fingers on the table. "The dean gave me Lancaster's name to substitute in for Professor Turner. He seems to be pretty close to the guy."

"I wonder who else he's close to." Uncle Pete scribbled a note. "Have you heard from your friend, Dante? Did he know this Lancaster?"

"Why would Dante try to shut down the retreat?" Cat could feel her anger building.

"That wasn't my question. I'm just wondering if you're in the middle of some family business we don't know about. The president seemed to think this was off the Covington radar, but this Lancaster guy's name is coming up more than I like." Uncle Pete snapped his notebook closed. "Has your friendly neighborhood gangster stopped by since he's been in town?"

"No." Cat saw Seth trying to pretend like he wasn't also waiting for her answer. "Guys, I haven't seen Dante in months. And the last time I did, I was walking home from town and he stopped me as I passed by his house. No big secret meetings. Do you really think Harriet's death could be about the families?"

Uncle Pete stood and put his hat on. "In Aspen Hills, a lot is about the families without us ever knowing. I'll check it out. Just stay clear of this Lancaster guy until I make sure he's not connected."

"I'll walk out with you," Seth said and followed her uncle out of the house.

Shauna leaned back in her chair. "So much for a perfect replacement for Professor Turner. I can't believe the little weasel was here, talking like a normal person, then goes and lies to your uncle. What's his game?"

Cat shook her head. "I don't know. But I'm going to find out."

Shauna shook her head. "Your uncle said to stay out of it."

"No, his exact words were 'don't talk to Lancaster.' I'm going to call the dean and see if this hearing can be cancelled now that Harriet's dead. I'll pretend like we didn't get the letter saying she'd been replaced. I want to hear it from the dean. Maybe then he can tell me why someone who he'd sent here, helping with the retreat, would be against it now. It's a valid question."

"If I hadn't opened the letter from the college yet, it's really the thing you would be doing. Especially if Lancaster didn't think your uncle would tell you about what he said."

"Or Lancaster might not know Pete's my uncle." Cat pulled out her phone. "Let's call now and see if we can catch the dean off guard."

She dialed the number to the dean's office by memory. Being a past Covington professor, Cat knew most of the English Department extensions by heart. Or if she didn't, she still had Michael's last employee phone directory tucked on a shelf in the den. As she waited for someone to answer, she played with the phone number she'd just dialed. Why did it seem so familiar? "Hi, is the dean available?"

The woman who'd answered the phone was probably a work study student. It was Thursday afternoon and the administration staff had their meetings on Thursdays. The professors met on Tuesdays, the deans of all the departments on Mondays. And no one with any power scheduled meetings on Fridays. That way professors and the higher ups could have a long weekend if they wanted. The scheduling never changed. Or hadn't since she was a teacher's assistant whose group always met on Fridays.

"May I help you?" the dean asked, clearly used to the lack of announcement when his real secretary was out of the office.

"Good afternoon, Dean. It's Cat Latimer. I was calling to see if you had reviewed my request to cancel the hearing about Covington's sponsorship of the retreat yet. I mean, with the untimely passing of Professor Barring, it's really not an issue anymore, is it?"

"Ms. Latimer, so nice to hear from you. We'd just received the paperwork for the scholarship you so generously sponsored under your late husband's name. I'm sure the money will help a great many people who want to study in the language arts." The dean continued to gush about the scholarship.

Cat really needed to call Dante and get a blow-by-blow on how he'd spent the money that the family had decided belonged to Michael for his work. She interrupted the listing of all the students who were actively studying in the field. "Sorry, no, I didn't call to talk about the scholarship and I'm sure you'll use it wisely."

"But, Ms. Latimer, per the scholarship instructions, you're the only one who can award the money. I'll have my secretary set us up a meeting to talk about its requirements."

"Sound great. I'm looking forward to working with you." She was going to kill Dante. "Anyway, back to my question. I'm planning some time in New York at my publishers' and noticed that the hearing was still on my calendar next week. Can we cancel that since, as far as I'm aware, Harriet was the only one opposed to Covington's sponsorship?"

"Cancel the hearing?" he repeated her request.

"That's my suggestion. Unless there are others who want to fight Harriet's battle." She paused for effect. "I'm sure, with the scholarship and all, you're not opposed to the retreat. Especially since so many of your past students have supported it, like Tom Cook."

"We've already replaced Harriet with a new professor to present her side." He dodged the question.

"Oh, who is that and why is he opposed to the retreat?" Cat knew sometimes you had to turn on the direct focus. Especially when the other person didn't want to answer the question.

"Look, let me look into it and see if there is a reason to continue with the hearing. I'm not sure if any of the professors are opposed to your retreat, at least not in the same way Harriet was."

"Great, then I'll hear back from you on Tuesday after the department meeting? That would be awesome."

"I'm not sure I can get it on the agenda by then."

Cat smiled at Shauna. "Well, I'm thinking you need to since the hearing is scheduled for next Thursday. It would be silly to put a discussion off until after the hearing, right? I'll just call you Tuesday at two. Or have your secretary put me on the calendar for then and we can finalize the scholarship terms at the same time. I'm writing it down now. Let me know if you want to do this over the phone or in person."

She hung up the phone and Shauna started to clap. "That was amazing."

"Thank goodness for Dante and his scholarship rules." She broke off to explain the set up to Shauna. "Although I hate him for setting me up this way. At least it gave me some power to force his hand." Cat tapped the table again. "But the dean didn't tell me who the other professor was. I wonder if he realized he'd made a mistake by putting Lancaster both in the retreat and on the hearing panel."

"I'm just glad I'm not on the other side from you," Shauna said.

Cat shrugged. "Uncle Pete told me to stop threatening to kill everyone I have a beef with, so I guess learning how to negotiate is a better skill than empty threats. Now, I'm heading upstairs to relax until dinner's ready, unless you need some help?"

"I'm not going to let you cook, Cat." Shauna walked over to her desk and held up a clipboard of things to do. "And it seems my list is all checked off except for dinner and refreshing the dining room before I head up to bed. Unless you need help with the sprinting group?"

"Actually, Deek said he'd handle it. So unless I wake up from a nap and just have a need to get words done, I think I'm done for the day." She stood and rolled her shoulders. "Maybe we should think about adding a hot tub to the back yard. I haven't felt this relaxed in months."

"It's the magical healing power of the hot springs water," Shauna called after her. "You can't get that out of the tap."

Cat pushed the door open and looked back. "I can try."

WHEN CAT AWOKE from the nap she'd taken after dinner, it was almost midnight. The house was quiet, but it didn't mean she was the only one up. Writers either wrote in the morning or late at night. There were a few who wrote during the normal nine-to-five workday, but since most of the writers she worked with were fitting it in around another job, they fit in the time to craft words when they could find slots in their schedule to sit down for a few minutes. One writer she knew wrote in fifteen-minute increments since she got a break in the morning, and one in the afternoon, and wrote at lunch around her day job. Then she either finished up her word count first thing in the morning or right after she finished working.

Writers were obsessed with getting the story down. It was just something they had to do to feel better. To feel like they were making progress. And to get the story out of their head. Sometimes, Cat wrote a short one- or two-page blurb about a book idea, just in case her agent came looking for another book idea. And it was usually a story that had been swirling around in Cat's head for a few weeks. That way, she didn't lose the idea, or if it wasn't going to work out, she could flesh out the idea while she worked the story. Sometimes things sounded better in her head.

She hadn't changed out of the yoga clothes she'd put on after going to the hot springs yet into pj's so she headed downstairs to the kitchen to see if the writers had left even one brownie in the dining room. If they hadn't, she'd grab a couple of cookies and a sparkling water to take back up to her room while she puttered around until she was tired again. If she didn't feel sleepy after thirty minutes of that, she'd go work in her office until her eyes started to close on their own. First, she checked the front door to make sure it was locked. It was. They left the foyer light on at night, just in case one of the writers wanted to go out or was coming back late. The grandfather clock in the foyer showed it was just before midnight.

The dining room didn't have any brownies so Cat combined the few cookies left on the sideboard onto one plate, then took a tray filled with dirty dishes into the kitchen. She was stacking the dishes in the sink when a light in the barn caught her eye. Either one of the writers or Shauna or maybe even Seth was out there.

She grabbed a flashlight by the door and slipped on a coat, putting the flashlight and a set of house keys in the pocket. She'd left her phone in her office, and she didn't feel like going all the way upstairs to get it. If there was something wrong, there was an extension in the barn she could use to call for help.

As Cat walked down the gravel path that Seth had put in from the back yard to the barn, an owl hooted in the distance. The light from the moon was bright enough so she didn't need to take out her flashlight. Pulling the coat closer, she knew winter would soon be overtaking the warm late fall days. Maybe Seth would be better so they could go cross country skiing this year. She knew he wouldn't be doing downhill this season. If they were even still a couple by then. They felt like a couple now, but there was a line that kept them from moving closer. Maybe it was the cancelled wedding. But really, Cat thought it was her fear that he'd leave again. She heard him saying he was done with missions, but hadn't he said it before too?

She was at the barn, and one of the kittens who were now full grown, Ali, came out to greet her. She picked him up and rubbed her face against his. He was warm. Apparently, he'd been inside until just now. She opened the barn door and saw a figure sitting on one of the hay bales, hunched over. She stepped into the barn and into the light. "Hello?"

The figure's head jerked up in fright and Cat could see that the figure was actually Stephen. And he'd been crying.

"What's going on?" Cat moved closer, hoping he'd recognize her.

His shoulders dropped when he saw it was her. "Sorry, I went for a walk and found myself here, where she died. She was a horrible person and our marriage was on the verge of falling apart, but there had been a time when we were just starting out that things were perfect. We met at Boise State University in English 202. I fell hard. And then we got married and moved here when she got a job at Covington. I started working at the community college, thinking that I'd get hired here, sooner or later. It didn't happen. Like kids, that didn't happen either."

"I'm sorry for your loss." Cat sat on a hay bale across from him. Snow, Shauna's horse whinnied softly from her stall.

"We would have divorced soon. Then I probably would have moved again. Maybe found someone new, maybe not. But that's not what hurts. I guess I'm grieving the life we could have had, not the one we actually did. The life we dreamed of as a young couple in a small apartment near campus." He wiped his face. "I know your uncle still thinks I killed Harriet. But I know I didn't and that's all I can control. That, and not being a jerk like I was yesterday morning."

She nodded and reached down to pet another cat who was winding through her legs, begging for attention. "I've had to learn the lesson of only dealing with what you can control as well. Several times."

A noise came from the doorway, Seth stood there, watching them. He met Cat's gaze. "Everything all right out here?"

"I was just about to head back in. Mind if I walk with you?" She stood and joined Seth at the door. She paused as she reached the doorway and turned back to Stephen. "Don't stay up too late. You've got a big day tomorrow as we start to close up the retreat."

When they were almost to the back yard, Seth spoke. "Are you sure that was safe?"

"I didn't know he was there when I went out to the barn. Just that there was a light on." Cat turned back to see the barn and the light coming out of the loft window. "I don't think he killed her."

"I'm glad because I would hate to think you were just sitting there, chatting up a killer about his regrets on his marriage." Seth turned on his flashlight as the moon went behind a cloud.

As they walked the last bit in silence, Cat thought about Stephen's regrets and if it had anything to do with Harriet's death. They needed to find out who she was meeting on the days Stephen was out of town. If they had that piece of information, she was certain they could find the actual killer.

And people would stop pointing fingers at her.

13

Cat slept through her alarm so she didn't have time to write before escorting the writers to the bookstore. The group was expected to be there at nine. Cat went into the kitchen to grab a travel mug to take coffee with her. She wasn't expected to stay for the session, by the time she'd finished with this coffee and had walked home, she should be awake enough to write. Or at least that was her plan.

"Good morning, sleepyhead." Shauna handed her a muffin sandwich with egg and cheese in it. It was wrapped up in paper towels. "Eat this and if you're still hungry when you get back, I can make you something else."

"This will work fine," Cat said before taking a bite of the sandwich. "I can't believe I slept in so late."

"That's what happens when you go exploring in the barn at midnight." Shauna shook a finger at her friend. "What were you thinking? If Seth hadn't been there..."

"Nothing was going to happen. Stephen didn't kill his wife. I'm sure of it. And since I didn't and Uncle Pete has no other suspects, this case just might not ever be solved." She took another bite of the sandwich before continuing. "This whole thing has to be about her job at Covington or maybe the clandestine meets she was having every Tuesday and Thursday when Stephen was out of town. I still think she was having an affair."

"I do too, but a letter and four digits isn't a lot to go on to figure out who she was seeing. But I believe that she must have been seeing more than one person." Shauna refilled her coffee and leaned against the counter. "I wonder if she had any friends at Covington who might talk to you."

"I'm a little person non gratis over there right now. Especially since I laid down the gauntlet with the dean yesterday." Cat took another bite of the sandwich. "This is really good."

"Thanks, I think. The way you scarfed it down, I don't think you've eaten in months," Shauna teased. "What about your friend from the English department? She still teaches at Covington, right?"

"Actually, no, they moved to Denver when she got offered a position with a new school. I think she wanted the fresh start. But she might know something about Harriet. Good call." Cat glanced at the clock. "I'll phone later today after I get some words in. I've got to go. The group should be waiting for me at the front door."

Shauna nodded toward the kitchen door. "Sounds like they're moving that way. Let me know if you're still hungry when you get home."

"Sadly, I'm always hungry. Which reminds me, I need to get back on the treadmill starting Sunday before none of my clothes fit." She moved toward the kitchen door. "See you soon."

"Watch for cars and look both ways," Shauna called after her as she walked out into the hallway.

Deek stood near the living room door, watching the stairs. She surprised him by walking out of the kitchen. "Oh, there you are. I was expecting you to come down from your office."

"The words are going to have to wait." Cat nodded toward the front door. "Time to get this show on the road."

"Before we leave, I wanted to make sure Stephen apologized. I mean, he told me he was going to do it, but sometimes he seems to be a little stubborn." Deek held up his hand. "I know, not my monkey or my circus, but he's a good guy. It's hard to be positive and upbeat when he's got so much going on, but he has moments."

"You're right, it's not your business." Cat paused before continuing, letting the words set in for Deek. "However, I can see you're serious, so yes, Stephen apologized. We're good."

Deek nodded but Cat could see the relief on his face. "I know I get too involved with people, but when I see their auras changing, I know they need some intervention. Otherwise, things can go bad."

"You read auras?" Cat had never met anyone who had that talent. Or, maybe she should say, who said they had that talent. She wasn't sure she was a believer in all the mystical stuff, but Deek seemed pretty normal. Well, besides his blond cornrows. "What do you mean, they can change? Are you saying someone can be normal or happy and then change to be a serial killer or something?"

"Maybe not that dramatic, but yeah, I've seen people's auras change and they've also changed their personalities. Maybe that's what I'm really seeing, is a person's personality." He nodded to the group. "Everyone over there is excited for the field trip. Including Dalton who you would think might be a little bored since he lives here."

"Well, we better get this show on the road then." Cat wasn't sure she really believed in Deek's gift, but as long as he wasn't hurting anyone or himself, she didn't see the harm in it. Besides, it might give him a different viewpoint to write from. And, as she moved everyone out of the house and toward the bookstore, she wondered if one of Tori's sorority friends might have the same talent. Which would give her an insight into the coven without being a member or actual witch.

She started a mental character sketch of this new addition to the books as they made their way to the bookstore. You never knew what was going to turn on a bright and shiny for an author. When they arrived at the bookstore, several of Tammy's writer group members were already there.

They were gathered around a table where a bunch of pictures

were spread out. Cat greeted Tammy at the counter and pointed over where now both sets of writers were gathering. "What's going on?"

"I made copies of the best of the pictures I took at the party. I had anyone who had a camera send me their picture too. There're two sets. Those—" she nodded to where the group had gathered— "and an extra copy for you and your writers. Please make sure they go through them before they leave Sunday and take what they want. Deek's in quite a few. He was very popular with our female members."

Cat laughed as she tucked the envelope into her pocket. "Thanks for doing this. I'll say goodbye to my group and get out of your hair."

"No problem. You know I love talking about books and bookselling. I'm just glad I didn't have to pack up all my writer books and drag them to your house. My arms thank you." Tammy called out and told the group to gather over in the area where she'd set up chairs. Cat knew the bookstore held their author events in the same general area, expanding or contracting as needed due to the size of the crowd.

"Hey, Warm Springs Writers? If you're wondering, Tammy got us a copy of all the pictures you saw on the table just now. I'll set them out in the living room on the back table and you can take what you want." Cat turned to Tammy. "Big thanks to Tammy and the bookstore for sponsoring this session and co-sponsoring the party. We need to do it again sometime."

"Definitely." Tammy gave Cat a hug and then went to stand by the lectern. "So welcome to my home away from home. I know as writers, you get the lure of a bookstore. I was born to the business as my parents owned the place before I took it over a few years ago."

Cat left the bookstore and stepped out into the chilly day. The smell of snow was in the air. Hopefully any storms would hold off until after Seth got back from Denver. The first snow of the season tended to be deep and luscious but caused the roads to be a little dicey until the snowplows and trucks got used to cleaning off the major roads. She'd check the weather report for the next few days when she got home. Or at least, after she got some words down on this new character and the chapter she wanted to write about how Tori found out about her friend's hidden talent.

When she got home, Shauna handed her a plate with a second sandwich. "Are you eating here or…"

Cat pointed at the door. "I had a brainstorm while walking the group to the bookstore. I need to get some of this down before the muse abandons me."

"Go play with your imaginary friends. I've got work to do anyway." Shauna turned back to the counter.

Cat pulled the envelope with the pictures out of her pocket. "Before I forget, can you set up a table in the living room to put these on? Tammy did a second copy of the pictures of the party. I'd like to have the guests take most of them home."

"Sure, but I'm pulling some for our marketing packet. I'll snap a picture of the ones I want then have Tammy send us the digital files. This was a fun idea. I should have thought of it." Shauna opened the envelope and started going through the snaps. "Oh, no. Do you want me to pull any of the pictures with Harriet?"

"You may want to send a copy to Uncle Pete, but otherwise, go ahead and leave them. They might be the last picture Stephen has of him and his wife." Cat paused at the doorway.

Shauna nodded, then added, "I just hope they aren't fighting in all of them."

"You and me both." Cat left the warm, inviting kitchen and headed upstairs to work. Her office was her sanctuary and she tried not to let worries go through that door. At least worries that weren't about the books. She had enough of them to keep herself busy there. She didn't need every day or retreat worries following her inside what should be her writing cave.

She turned on the computer, found her document and started writing, making hand-written notes in her series notebook in pen when she made decisions like character names and descriptions. It helped keep her organized and she didn't have to remember decisions she'd already made.

Cat closed out the files about three. She hadn't stopped for lunch and she was starving again. She stood and stretched. Shauna had stocked her mini fridge with granola bars and sodas so she just pulled from there when she needed something. Especially on days where the writing was flowing, like today.

She went down to the kitchen and had put a bowl of soup in the microwave and was waiting for it to warm up when she remembered the pictures. She wanted to see them before the writers took their favorites. She grabbed a soda and headed into the living room.

She sorted through the pictures, setting aside one of her and Shauna as well as one with her and Seth. She was almost finished when another one caught her eye. A woman in a zombie outfit with her hair sticking out. Shauna had the description down correctly. The zombie stood with her arm around a man in an old-fashioned safari outfit. He was looking at her and laughing as the woman took an attack position obviously for the camera. She didn't recognize the woman, but she did recognize the man. It was Professor Todd Lancaster. She'd seen him in the crowd that night, but hadn't taken the time to go visit. He must have seen the flyer that she'd put up on the announcement board in the teachers lounge.

But who was the woman in the zombie outfit?

She stood looking through the pictures again, trying to see if there were any others showing either Professor Lancaster or the woman. She'd gathered three total when the writers showed up from wherever they'd been. They poured into the living room and gathered around her.

"These are so cool!" Pixie held up one of her in the sprite costume. "I'm blowing this one up for my wall."

"Egomaniacal much?" Cari teased as she went through the photos.

Cat held up the picture of Lancaster and the zombie woman. "Did anyone talk to either of these people at the party?"

Stephen stepped over, a picture of him and Harriet in his hand. Somehow the photographer had caught them in a happy moment. They were laughing and Stephen was looking at her, the love apparent on his face. "That's Todd and Jessi Lancaster. I figured you knew him since he came and talked Tuesday. Maybe you didn't recognize him in his costume."

"I saw Todd, but I've never met his wife." Cat looked around the group. No one else had responded to the picture. "Does she work at the college?"

"She's in administration. Something about student aid?" He pulled the picture closer. "I always thought they were a cute couple. I tried to get Harriet to set up some double dates, but she didn't want to have to make small talk with someone who did numbers for a living."

"Oh." Cat wasn't sure how to respond.

Stephen grimaced. "I know, it makes her sound snobby. And she was, but I still loved her. I guess I didn't care as long as she didn't mind making small talk with me."

"You love who you love." Cat nodded to the picture in his hand. "You have a nice memory there."

He smiled as he held it closer to see it again. "We look happy. I'm going to get if framed. It will be a lovely reminder of the good times. Which there were many."

Cat watched as he walked away. Then she called out to the group. "Okay, we'll start the last session tonight at six thirty. Here's the plan for the next couple of days. We'll talk about the retreat tonight. What worked for you, what didn't. Things like that. Then we'll do a few rounds of word sprints. Update your word count on the board no later than three pm tomorrow and then the winner will be announced at our dinner Saturday night. We'll leave at five to get to the restaurant. It's upscale Mexican flavors and casual dress but you can dress up or down. It's date night around here so you'll see people wearing all sorts of outfits."

Pixie giggled and bounced a bit. "I've got the perfect dress. Maybe I'll meet a cowboy who will come rescue me in California and bring me back to live on his ranch."

"I think that's called kidnapping nowadays," Cari said and the room broke into laughter.

The group had bonded. Even with a murder, or maybe because of one. But Cat was thankful either way. Part of the magic of the retreat was making new writer friends. If they took this path on to being their career, they would need some people they could trust. And laugh with.

She headed into the kitchen to see if Shauna had already sent some of the pictures to Uncle Pete. Cat had three more to send.

Shauna was mixing a batch of brownies when Cat entered the kitchen. And from the smell, she already had one batch in the oven. "Hey, I was just about to come up and see if you were coming down or not. I heard the guests come in the front."

"They are in looking over the pictures. I was in there when they arrived." Cat laid the three pictures of Todd Lancaster and his wife on the table. "Did you see these?"

"Hold on a second." Shauna poured the batter into the oiled pan and put the bowl in the sink, turning on the water to fill it. She dried her hands on a towel and stepped closer to the table. "That's the zombie I saw with Todd. It's his wife, right? Are they from Tammy's writers' group?"

"No, I think Todd saw the flyer and he brought his wife as a plus one." Cat sank into a chair. "We need to send these to Uncle Pete as well."

"Yeah, our friend Todd is showing up all over the place. And I'm not sure, but maybe those zombie clothes were what Harriet was found in." Cat took her phone out and snapped pictures of each photo, then sent the group in a text to her uncle. "I'll let the professionals figure that one out."

They talked for a few minutes, then Cat's phone rang.

"Why is the professor who claims you killed Harriet at your party with a zombie?" Uncle Pete asked.

"Our Professor Lancaster brought his wife to the party," Cat responded, then saw Shauna's frown. "I left an invite on the bulletin board at the school for all the English department professors. I didn't expect anyone to really come. I just want them to know we were having a party and be jealous."

"Sometimes I think you ask to be in hot water all the time." Uncle Pete sighed. "Thanks for sending these. Now we have a reason to go back and talk to more people. I like having an active investigation with more people than my niece in the suspect pool."

He hung up the phone leaving her to wrestle with that last statement. He hadn't let her ask if those were the clothes that Harriet was found in.

Shauna turned off her buzzer and took the first batch of brownies out. "What did he say?"

There were so many answers for that, but Cat kept it simple. "He said thank you."

14

The group gathered early in the living room. When Cat came out of the kitchen with Seth at six, they were already there, talking. He nodded to the doorway. "Do you need to go? Sam will understand if you can't stop by and rub his tummy tonight."

Cat laughed as she opened the door to the west wing. "They're just spending some last quality time together. They don't need me for a few minutes. Besides, I miss my Sambo."

The dog must have heard her voice because he came running to greet her. With a quick, "sit," from Seth, Sam responded, plopping on his butt right in front of Cat. His tail sped back and forth on the floor.

Seth laughed as Cat reached down to pet him. "As you can see, I no longer have to sweep or vacuum. I just let Sam do the work. Come on, Sam, let Cat in so we can go out to the deck. I think it's warm enough this afternoon for that."

Cat followed Seth and Sam to the back door off the kitchen. "It won't be for long. Do you have a coat?"

He grabbed a parka off the railing where several coats hung. "Here you go. And yes, as soon as the sun sets at six fifteen, it's going to start cooling down."

"I think we're going to get snow early next week," Cat said after they got outside. She'd sat on one of the deck chairs, but Seth was standing and throwing a ball to Sam, over and over.

"I heard that too. Hopefully we'll get these guys out of here and flying back to always sunny California." He took the ball that Sam had dropped at his feet and threw it again. "I wonder what couples talk about in California when they're fighting. It can't be the weather. It would be a really short conversation."

Cat laughed as she turned to look at him. "I think it's going to be sunny today. No rain in the forecast."

"Yeah, we sure could use some rain." Seth followed her lead. "Maybe next week."

"Maybe that's why they have marriage counseling, to give couples a common topic," Cat added.

"Common as in how much we both hate this counselor?" Seth threw the ball again, then came over and sat down. "Monday, we can grab some takeout for lunch, then go park at the trailhead and talk."

She nodded but then smiled. "If it doesn't snow."

"My truck has four-wheel drive." Seth clicked his fingers when Sam brought the ball again. Sam lay on the deck, the ball still in his mouth. "If the weather is horrible, we'll have lunch with Shauna then come over to this wing and talk. I love you, Cat. That's not going to change."

Tears stung her eyes. "I just can't start this. I have a meeting in a few minutes."

"I know and I don't want you to look like a racoon, so stop crying." When she chuckled, he nodded to the sun going behind the mountain. "Just sit and take in that view. We're lucky people to be able to live here. You have to count your blessings every day."

Seth was right; the view was breathtaking and worth the few minutes it took out of her busy day. She needed to do this more. "We need to order a hot tub and set it right here."

"Just for us?" He winked at her.

She felt the blush settle on her cheeks. "Well, not for the writers. It might distract them from what they need to get done. A week isn't a lot of time to pack in a years' worth of creativity."

His watch beeped and he groaned. "Time for you to go inside and become a pumpkin. Have fun with your writers. Shauna said you might have a new suspect for Pete to check out?"

She stood and brushed off her pants. "Lancaster's wife was clearly at the party from the picture we have, and in an actual zombie costume. As long as it matches what we found on Harriet's body, it's a no-brainer."

"But if it doesn't fit? Like the trial with the glove in a certain celebrity spouse killing?" Seth asked, rubbing Sam's belly as he talked. "Besides, it's circumstantial. She might have changed out of the outfit and threw it away. Maybe someone got it out of her trash."

"Then we're right back to the few suspects, including me, and I'd rather not be on that exclusive list." Cat moved toward the door. "If anything, it gives Uncle Pete something else to look at. I'm still not certain that it's not all about Covington. You know they take care of things in a different way there."

"If it was a Covington thing, Harriet would have disappeared, not be stuffed in your barn for someone to find." Seth took the ball from Sam. "You know they don't like loose ends."

Cat paused at the door. "Are you coming in?"

Seth threw the ball across the yard. "In a few minutes. Sam needs some exercise."

Cat went inside, brushing her shoes on the rug by the door and hanging up his coat on the hook. She glanced out the window for a minute, watching Sam chase the ball and bring it to his master. Sam liked her. He loved Seth.

Moving through the living room, the cover of a book caught her eye. It was sitting by Seth's chair. She opened it to the bookmark and read a few sentences. Her latest Tori release. She hadn't known Seth to ever read anything she'd written. Yet here was proof he was reading the last book she'd published. She tucked the bookmark into the book and set it on the table.

She looked toward the kitchen to make sure he hadn't followed her inside. "Seth Howard, you are a mystery."

Then she left the west wing and headed up to her office to grab her Friday night session folder and her laptop, just in case she decided to write with the group after the meeting. Her head was filled with memories of her and Seth, and not for the first time, she wondered why she was even mad. The memory of the sleepless nights when he was out of country returned and the fear of losing him forever slapped her in the face. Why was she making sure he couldn't hurt her again when he hadn't tried to hurt her in the first place?

She pushed her emotions into the "after the retreat" box and opened the door to her office. She liked the imagery of stepping into her working world. It was why she mostly wrote in her office except for retreat weeks. That way the "writing Cat" and the real-life Cat had a dividing point. Mostly it worked so she didn't worry about the writing when she wasn't upstairs actively working. But sometimes, the answer to a writing block or a missed plot step would hit her at the oddest times. She made sure she had notebooks all over the house. That way, she could jot down the solution without running the three sets of stairs to her office.

Work-life balance was a nice concept, but when you worked at home, sometimes the lines tended to fade together. She made a note before she left about the January editing retreat and having a session on work-life balance. Most writers fit their writing into the nooks and crannies of their lives. Which was how things got done, but what about life? She wondered if there were any social science or psychology professors working on the concept at Covington. Which might be a second way of getting the access she needed if the English department failed her.

She grabbed her notebook, laptop, and the retreat file she'd put together with the writers' goals as well as a few concluding remarks she always liked to say. There would be more time tomorrow at the dinner, but she wanted that to be fun and light.

Or at least as fun as it could be with an active murder investigation going on. She opened the file and looked at Stephen's goal list. He had a word count listed as well as a few research projects he wanted to start, and under the personal goals, he wrote one thing. *Start to learn to live without Harriet.*

Cat didn't believe Stephen had killed his wife. But Uncle Pete didn't have a lot of suspects on the list. She hoped this new information about Lancaster and his wife being at the party would open up the suspect pool. Her watch buzzed. She had five minutes before the last session would start.

Putting aside the murder, it had been a good session so far in her eyes. The party had allowed the writers a faster bond. Except three of them had already known each other. So she couldn't totally call that a result. The Covington student had bonded well with the group. And their last-minute addition hadn't caused the group dynamics to change much. Either Cat and Shauna were getting better at this retreat thing, or the mix of people had made it work.

She thought it was probably the latter.

When she walked in the living room, the group was brainstorming. She dropped her stuff on her chair and tapped Deek's arm from his place next to her. "I'm grabbing some coffee. I'll be right back."

"Oh, wow, I can't believe it's that late already." Deek stood and addressed the group. "Hey, it's almost time for our session. Pixie? Are you good with the title suggestions you got or should we meet tomorrow morning to finish this up?"

"I'm good. I'm going to play around with a few, but yeah, I think I have some good options here." Pixie ripped the flipchart paper off the stand. "I need some sustenance. I wonder if there's more brownies."

"I'm sure there are." Cat smiled at the group as they all stood and stretched. "You guys are rocking this group participation section of the retreat. I'm going to have to give you all A's."

"Wait, are we going to have a grade after this?" Cari's face went pale. "I should have been writing more."

"I was just kidding, but seriously, most groups don't bond this fast or take over the retreat as much as you guys did. So thank you. I wasn't worried about your success at the retreat at all." Cat glanced at her watch. "We'll meet back here in five?"

"My mom used to say that you get what you give out of life,"

Stephen said as they moved from the living room into the hallway. "But I'm pretty sure she didn't know how much more you can experience when you just let people into your world."

Deek slapped him on the back. "Dude, you've had a stressful week, yet you still showed up every day. I'd be curled in a ball somewhere if I had to live through your week."

Stephen smiled and then moved to the stairs. "I'll be right back. Save me a brownie, would you?"

Deek and Cat were the last ones left in the hallway. Deek turned to Cat. "He does seem like he's doing good, right? It's just not me."

Cat turned to look at the stairs, a frown forming on her face. "No, I think Stephen is doing really well considering everything that happened."

"Deek, get in here. Shauna made that pecan cookie you loved so much." Pixie called out from the dining room.

Cat smiled before she turned around. No use showing her concern. Deek was already worried about his new friend. "I love those cookies too."

The group was back in the room in ten minutes, not five, but they all had treats in front of them. Some had coffee, some hot cocoa, and some water. They had their notebooks open and pens ready. It was time to finish up the learning part of the retreat.

"I used to do this session on Saturday afternoon before our dinner, but then you had no time to finish up any thoughts that this session brought up. This session isn't here to make sure you hit your goals this week." Cat passed out the original sheets they'd done Monday morning to each attendee. She had copies in her office for future planning processes. "Even if you didn't hit your goals, we need to talk about ways you can take the retreat home."

"I can just quit my job and move in here. I'm sure I can find a way to pay for my keep." Pixie raised her hand. "Shauna can teach me to cook."

"I've tasted your cooking. I'm not sure even Shauna can help you," Deek teased and got a pen thrown at him for his effort.

"They say there's no bad ideas in brainstorming, but let's frame out the guidelines a little better." Cat smiled at Pixie. She was going to miss this group. Cat stood and grabbed one of the markers. "Without any of you staying here forever, what are some ways you can take this retreat home with you and make sure your writing self has a seat at your table. So to speak."

Ideas started flowing then and Cat wrote them on the board as they floated up from the guests. "Write every day. Set aside a writing desk or area. Find friends to sprint with when needed. Trust your muse. Write when you're not inspired. Write with a timer. Keep a word count. Try new things."

Deek held up his hand. "I think we're all in one except Dalton, but I'd like to add join a writing group."

"Dude, my entire college experience is a writing group." Dalton turned toward him. "What else do you want from me?"

Cat jumped in. "I see what Deek's saying. Dalton, in your classes, you're writing poetry or analyzing writing. If you really want to finish this paranormal book, you need a group where you can talk about the fiction writing. It can't be a secret."

Dalton squirmed in his chair. "I don't know. If the department found out, they'd make fun of me. Maybe worse."

"Maybe. But as long as you're doing the work, they can't mess with your scholarship. What about Tammy's writers' group? Stephen, you're in that. Would Dalton being there raise red flags for anyone?"

Stephen shook his head. "They're all really nice. They knew about Harriet and her not wanting me to write. And they kept my secret. Most of the people there don't work at Covington. But some of us, like Jessi Lancaster and me, we have spouses at Covington. It's a joke with us that we're like a secret gathering."

"Jessi Lancaster? Todd, Professor Lancaster's wife?" Cat tried to make her voice sound normal, but this was another reason Todd had been at the party.

"Yeah. Neither he nor Harriet were excited to attend the party, but I guess we both were pretty persuasive. At least they had each other to complain to while the rest of us had fun." Stephen turned back to Dalton. "We meet on Wednesday nights at seven. Come try it out. If you don't like it or feel comfortable, you can leave, but I think you'll love it. It's good to have people who understand you."

Cat wrote down Deek's suggestion and then opened the floor again. "Other ways?"

"Goal setting," Cari added. "I'm pretty driven and I thought I was getting stuff done, but when I made a specific word count goal for each day, no matter what, it made a huge difference in my output."

They continued for a few more minutes, then Cat handed out another piece of paper. "This is your contract with future you. Write down at least three things you're going to do starting on Monday to keep experiencing the retreat process at home. Writing them as goals will give you better control of when you've met them and you can make new ones. You should review your goals at least weekly and adjust monthly."

"But word count is daily, right?" Pixie frowned at the paper.

Cat shrugged. "Maybe. If you have a job where you can't write certain days, maybe your count is weekly so you can carve out little bits of time during the day or the week. It all depends on your schedule."

"And how bad you want it," Dalton said. He stared at the paper. "It's like we're building our own writing class where we make the rules and grade ourselves. I can be in school forever without paying tuition or getting student loans."

Cat laughed at the imagery but nodded. "The best thing about being a writer is you get to be a lifetime learner. Publishing changes, book trends change, you change. And it's all reflected in your writing. Dalton's right, get ready to have homework for the rest of your life."

"Some people would hate that," Deek said as he wrote down his goals. "For me, it sounds like heaven. So who's wrong?"

"Neither one of you. You both just found your passion," Cat said.

The evening continued with a few rounds of writing sprints. After the second one, Cat felt worn out and called it a night. As she made her way out of the room, Stephen called her name and met up with her in the hallway.

"I just wanted you to know that Harriet's funeral is tomorrow at nine so I'll be out of the retreat for most of the morning. I'm not doing a wake at the house but there's a reception thing at the church after the service that I'll need to attend. You guys are welcome to come but you don't have to. I told the group about it earlier and asked them not to come on my behalf. I'd rather spend time with them here tomorrow afternoon talking about writing and life. The funeral, well, it's about Harriet." He wiped a spare tear from his face. "Does that make sense?"

"We'll be there and represent the retreat for you." Cat placed her hand on Stephen's arm. "You've been really strong here considering all you've gone through."

"Besides being a horrible person to you the other day." Stephen smiled and nodded. "I think I kept it together pretty well. And thanks for the after the retreat plan. This is going to be my lifeline once I go back to our house."

"You're always welcome here for a cup of coffee and some writing talk if you need it," Cat added.

Stephen turned back to the living room. "I might take you up on that. Anyway, I need to get in there before they start without me. They hate it that I can write faster than any of them."

Cat went into the kitchen to see if Shauna and Seth were there. As she suspected, they were both there waiting for her group to finish.

"How did it go?" Shauna asked.

"Good. We've almost got another retreat in the bag." Cat went to the stove and made herself a cup of tea. "Do you want to go to Harriet's funeral tomorrow with me? Stephen just asked if we could make it."

"Are we going to support Stephen or look for possible suspects?" Seth asked.

Cat sat down with her cup. She dumped the bag back and forth several times as she thought about the answer. Finally, she decided to be honest. "Both?"

15

Uncle Pete was already at the church when Cat and Shauna came into the vestibule the next morning. He excused himself from the conversation with Mark the funeral home director who was also the county coroner. Mark waved at Cat and Shauna, then disappeared into a doorway that must have led to a separate room.

Cat scanned the small crowd but didn't see Stephen. Todd Lancaster was on the other side of the room, standing with the woman who Stephen had identified as Todd's wife, by his side. He was talking to the dean. They looked up and saw Cat watching them. Again, she got a slight smile from the men and a wave before Todd took his wife's arm and the trio disappeared into the chapel.

"Man, I'm just clearing out the room," Cat muttered before her uncle got close. Shauna frowned and looked around but Cat could tell she hadn't seen the funeral director or the Covington group. "Uncle Pete, I'm glad to see a friendly face. Stephen asked us to come, but I don't see him anywhere."

"He's in a room with the body— I mean, saying goodbye to his wife." Uncle Pete groaned. "It's hard to change up the terminology when I'm not on the job."

"I won't tell anyone." She hugged him. "You look tired. Did you hire anyone yet?"

"I've got a temp settled in but that woman had rearranged everything and took our ordering process off automatic restocking, so the new girl has had to go through and set everything back the way it was. That will teach me to release control over things without making sure the new hire is going to stay."

"And not be crazy about you," Shauna added. "Pete, you just have to realize you're a catch. Especially for women of a certain age looking for a partner who isn't hanging at the bar or running in every fun run available."

"Hey, Michael ran in those marathon things," Cat protested.

Shauna raised her eyebrows. "And look how that turned out."

Cat laughed, then covered her mouth when people looked over at her. "Not because he liked to run. Anyway, Uncle Pete, I'm glad you got her out of there before she could do some real damage to your relationship. I like Shirley."

"Funny thing, I do too." He held up a hand, then dug in his pocket, pulling out a baggie with what looked like a diamond earring inside. "The crime lab boys found this in the barn. I just talked to Stephen, and he said Harriet didn't like posts. She was more of a dangling earring type. And, he knows she had these black caldrons on Saturday night to go with the costume. Is this either of yours?"

Cat reached up to make sure both the diamonds that Seth had given her for Christmas a few years ago were still in her ears. "I only have one pair of diamond earrings and I'm wearing them right now. Shauna?"

She peered at the diamond. "The ones that Kevin gave me are in my safety deposit box. I have some lab cut ones I wear occasionally, but they are round cut. These are marquise cut. Not mine." Shauna had been engaged to Kevin a few years ago. The man had everything, but he'd been killed right after they'd announced their engagement.

"I suppose Seth hasn't been bringing women over to the barn, lately, has he?" Uncle Pete took the baggie back.

"What am I being blamed for now?" Seth stepped next to Cat and held out his hand. "I was parking the car. Nice to see you, Pete."

"Seth." Pete shook his hand. "You don't know where this earring belongs, do you?"

Seth took the baggie and peered at it. He glanced at Cat who shook her head. "It's not really my style."

"We haven't had any visitors to the barn lately, right?" Cat asked, already knowing the answer. Sometimes they had inspectors come in to check Seth's work, but the barn remodel was done a couple of years ago. "Maybe it's been there a while?"

"The crime tech log has it close to the door and in the middle of the floor. I've sent a picture to the EMTs and my guys, but they don't usually wear jewelry on a crime scene. Just for this reason." Uncle Pete tucked the baggie back into his pocket. "If you think of any explanation, let me know. Otherwise, it might be a clue to the killer."

"You think the killer might be female?" Cat asked, knowing the answer would put her back on the suspect list, if she had ever been off anyway.

"Or a guy who likes nice jewelry. Either way, it limits our pool. They did DNA testing on it before they released it back to the evidence locker. I thought this might be a good time to see if anyone claims it or had seen it on someone." He looked up as the music changed and the funeral director now stood in front of the chapel doorway. "Time for this party to get started. Do you want to sit together?"

Cat took his arm. "That would be lovely. Thank you."

He smiled down at her. "Anytime. Just don't go off interviewing suspects at the coffee service afterwards. I can't really run to chase anyone down in these shoes."

"I'm sure you have at least one officer posted outside, watching the place." Cat moved toward the chapel with her uncle. Seth and Shauna followed behind. She'd married Michael in this same church. Small town churches were like that. They held memories of baptisms, childhood, marriage, and finally, the goodbye ceremonies. We are a ritualistic society, Cat thought as they found a pew near the front and slipped into it. Seth sat down next to her and took her hand in his.

She squeezed it, letting him know she was all right. And the service began.

Several people from the college spoke about Harriet's life at work. How passionate she was about passing on the heritage of the literary works of the greats. And that she'd be missed for her professional works. No one talked about Harriet, the woman. Finally, Stephen stood and approached the lectern. He unfolded a paper to read from and tried to press out the wrinkles. Finally, he looked up at the church full of people.

"I want to thank everyone who came to honor Harriet today. She would have loved to have heard all your comments and how she'd made a difference in your lives. Harriet was the love of my life. We'd met in college and we were together ever since. Even though Harriet told me under no certain terms that even though we were married, she would never give up her work to play housewife for me."

The audience chuckled. Apparently, that had been a common statement they'd heard from her as well.

"I never asked her to make that sacrifice. When we couldn't have kids, we thought it was a blessing. We were both too busy with work to step back. I would have made a horrible father. I can't keep a house plant alive." Stephen paused and looked down to his notes. "Harriet wasn't perfect, but she was perfect for me and our lives. And I guess, that's all that matters. Thank you all for coming."

Cat watched as Stephen stepped off the altar and almost fell back into his spot on the pew. The minister came up and asked for a moment of prayer. After a few additional verses and songs, the funeral was over, and the minister asked everyone to gather in the back for some refreshments.

After she said goodbye to Uncle Pete, Cat and the others moved into the reception hall next to the chapel. She scanned the area and spotted Stephen sitting by himself, a cup of coffee next to him at the table. Two cookies sat on a plate. She didn't see the dean or Todd and his wife in the sparse crowd. She turned to Seth and Shauna.

"Let's let Stephen know we're leaving and remind him about the dinner tonight. It looks like he could use some people around him to cheer him up a little." Cat leaned a little closer to Seth. What was it about funerals that made the living remember what it meant to be alive?

"Sounds like a plan. I'll go get the car. I had to park down the street at that park; the lot for the church was full." Seth squeezed her elbow gently and pointed toward the front door. "I'll be at the front in five minutes at the latest. It should get pretty busy here and I'd like to beat the traffic. I need to feed Sam still."

"We'll be there." Cat nodded to where Stephen sat. "Come on, let's say our condolences and wait for Seth by the front door."

Shauna stood by her side when they reached the table. She cleared her throat and Stephen looked up. "I'm so sorry for your loss."

"Hi, I'm so glad you all came." He scanned the room. "You're one of only a few friendly faces. You'd think your uncle had already charged me with Harriet's murder."

"They just don't know what to think." Cat squeezed Stephen's shoulder. "Thanks for inviting us. Seth's getting the car. I'm sorry we have to leave so soon, but it's the final day of the retreat, and I like to be there for last-minute questions."

"I'm just glad you came. It made the day a little less bleak. I'll be back at the house as soon as they release me from this hell." He nodded as someone Cat didn't know came up to speak with him. "Vern, thank you for coming."

Cat and Shauna headed to the front door to wait for Seth. As they stood there, Cat couldn't shake the thought that she'd seen that earring before. But where?

"I thought it was nice that Stephen had the memorial donations go to the Covington scholarship fund for graduate students." Shauna stood by the window in the little covered porch where she could watch for the car. "So much better than just letting all those flowers die. When Kevin died, I sent all the flowers to the hospital so they could put them in patient rooms."

"Yeah, because nothing says *get well soon* better than funeral arrangements," Cat teased, but her mind was still on that stupid earring and where she'd seen it.

"I'm sure they took off the cards. Flowers are flowers. When I went to church with my grandmother, the arrangement from funerals that had been held at that church stayed there for the next Sunday service. The minister always mentioned how nice it was of the family to donate them. I guess the flower budget for services must get a little overwhelming." Shauna pointed to the street. "I see the car right there."

"Speaking of flowers, did you thank Linda Cook for the two dozen roses? Or is it my turn?" Cat followed her down the sidewalk where they could meet Seth. Linda was the widow of an author who had attended and died at the first Warm Springs Writers' Retreat. She sent flowers every month even though Cat had told her it was unnecessary. She had told Cat that it was a nice way for her to keep Tom, her late husband, on her mind.

"It was your turn, but I handled it since you've been busy with the retreat, the writing, and well, Seth." She opened the back door to the SUV. She waited until Cat got in the car, then leaned forward. "Thanks for the door-to-door service. We could have walked to the park with you."

Seth laughed and caught her gaze in the rear-view mirror. "Cat, yes, but you couldn't walk a block in those heels. Besides, it got me out of there early. I swear, funerals are the worst."

Cat didn't say anything until they got back to the house. When Seth went to the other wing to take care of Sam, she sat at the table rather than heading upstairs to change clothes.

Shauna put on a kettle for tea and got out two cups. "It looks like you want to chat."

Cat shrugged. "I wanted to thank you for taking care of everything."

"Emailing Linda wasn't hard. I like chatting with her." Shauna put tea bags in the cups and as the water heated up, sat down at the table with Cat.

Cat shook her head. "I don't mean that. Or not, just that. You do so much around here. The retreat wouldn't be a success without you. I don't think I say that enough. I get a lot of thanks from the guests since I'm the author attached to the retreat and I work with them more. You do a lot around here. I just wanted to say thank you."

"You're welcome." The kettle blew and Shauna stood to finish their tea. "I have to admit I'm loving this adventure. When I moved here from California, I thought it would be at most a six-month thing. I'd get bored and quit or you'd find out you hated me and kick me out. Instead, it's been a joy. I've learned a lot about myself and my passion for cooking. And we've helped a lot of writers. So thank you for bringing me along with you."

Cat held up the cup of tea. "To many more years of retreats."

"Don't sip that tea yet, it's hot," Shauna said, but clicked her cup to Cat's. "To many more years."

After finishing her tea and finalizing the logistics for the night's dinner, Cat ran upstairs and changed. Then she wandered into the living room. She'd given the writers until three to update their counts and someone, probably Deek, had made a flip chart listing the writers' names with room for word counts on an hourly basis. Pixie was checking in hourly, but Deek, Dalton, and Cari were less frequent. The only one who hadn't added in words was Stephen, who was still at the church. Cat took her phone and took a picture of the goals board. She drew a star on Deek's name. As of last night, he was ahead, but not by much. Looking at today's listing, any one of the others could probably catch him, except for Stephen. He just didn't have the time to write that many words.

She tucked the phone into her jeans pocket and then walked through the rest of the room. The table with the pictures was still set up and Shauna had made a sign to take as many as you want. Cat started setting up the pictures in a more organized fashion. Yes, she was a touch OCD, but she wondered if that was her writing style controlling the other parts of her life. She wrote better when her mind was organized, and she needed her life to be organized as well.

She came upon a picture of Todd and his wife. They were smiling at the camera, even if his arm around her seemed a little protective, maybe even controlling. She wondered what that picture said about their relationship, if anything. She moved a picture of her and Seth next to the other couple. She and Seth, even though they were having problems, seemed more open. The smiles less staged or forced. As she leaned over to closer examine the wife's face, Cat froze. She picked the picture up and ran to the kitchen.

Shauna sat reading a book, a full cup of tea in front of her. She set the book down when she saw Cat come in. "What's wrong?"

Cat set the picture on the table. "Is it my imagination or are those the earrings that Uncle Pete has in the evidence bag? Or at least one of them."

Shauna picked up the picture and closely reviewed the picture. "We need to send this to Pete."

"I thought you already sent him pictures."

Shauna went to the desk and grabbed her laptop. "He probably has it, but I want to make sure. Because he didn't pick up on the earring, now did he?"

Cat texted her uncle to let him know that Shauna had sent the email. There was no response. "I wonder if he's taking a nap."

"We just saw him at the funeral." Shauna closed the laptop. "We've done everything we can do. Now it's up to Pete. Let him do his job."

The door to the kitchen opened and Pixie stepped inside. "Hey, Cat, do you mind meeting with us a minute? We've got some questions. And you too, Shauna."

"We'll be right there. Are you guys in the living room?"

Pixie nodded. "We've been talking about the retreat and have some follow-up questions from what you said on Thursday."

Cat stood and rolled her shoulders. "And just like that, we're back to work. I wonder why they want you to come too?"

"Recipes probably." Shauna picked up a copy of her book. "I'm just going to smile and hold this up. Maybe I should get a recipe card for one of the book's recipes, then put the vendor links on the back."

"Put the retreat's website on the back too and I'll approve it as a marketing expense." Cat held the door open for Shauna. "I love the creativity that comes out of our retreat weeks."

When they reached the living room door, it was closed. Cat frowned and pushed the door open.

"Surprise!" a chorus of voices called out. The room that had been set up for the retreat just a few minutes ago was now filled with balloons and a very large cake.

Deek was the first to greet them. "I know you're taking us to dinner as our thank you for coming to the retreat, but we wanted to return the favor with more food. So here's a thank you for holding the retreat. We know it's not easy and you all have busy lives besides the retreat, so thank you for giving us this gift."

Stephen started clapping and then the group joined in. She heard clapping behind her and Seth walked into the room.

"Seth, you were supposed to come in with the others," Pixie called out. "I told you to hurry."

"Darling, this is my hurry speed. I still get some cake, right?" Seth put an arm around Cat. "I think your writer friends are a pretty amazing bunch."

Cat looked around the room and nodded. "I couldn't agree more."

16

They were just finishing the cake when Uncle Pete came into the living room. He looked around at the balloons and streamers. "Did I miss a birthday?"

"Hey, Pete, do you want chocolate or white cake? Or one of the border pieces that have both?" Seth picked up the cake cutter. "I didn't even know they made cake this way."

"I'll take chocolate with vanilla ice cream." He moved over to Cat. "I came in through the kitchen, but no one was there."

"Sorry, the writers threw an end of retreat thank you party for us." Cat looked around at the group eating and talking together. "This is the first time this has happened, right, Shauna?"

Shauna wiped her mouth with a napkin. "These guys are the best. I'm going to miss them on Monday morning."

Uncle Pete took the plate and spoon Seth had given him. "Cat, I hate to pull you away from the party, but can we talk in the kitchen?"

"Is it news?" Stephen came up next to them. "May I be allowed to hear it?"

Uncle Pete nodded. "I guess it's not a secret. Or it won't be in the morning."

"Then let's just talk here." Stephen nodded to the group. "They've been a part of this since the party and well, after Harriet was found. They all should know if you've found the killer."

Cat nodded when her uncle looked at her for permission.

He sat down on the wing chair and set the plate on the coffee table. "Okay then, here's the story. Cat and Shauna sent me the pictures of Todd and Jessi Lancaster at the party. I'd already asked them about her zombie costume, but she swore she'd thrown hers away as soon as they got home that night. Todd even said he'd seen her put it in the trash and that their trash collectors came the next day."

"Did you send people to the refuse place to try to find it?" Seth asked, clearly involved in the story. "Because yuck."

Uncle Pete chuckled. "And that's just what my people said when I sent them there. It was pretty much a wash since what we'd be trying to prove was it wasn't in the trash pile. And we didn't find it. I've got the lab working on it but I'm pretty sure it's the one we found on Harriet. Surprisingly, the two women were almost the same size. And the clothes were oversized."

"So a negative of a negative doesn't always prove a positive," Deek said.

"Exactly." Uncle Pete beamed at Deek like he'd said something totally not crazy.

Cat, on the other hand, was still confused. "Wait, so you can't prove Jessi or Todd killed Harriet? Are we back at square one?"

"No, I couldn't prove it, but now, thanks to the picture and my discussion with the lovely couple—who threw each other in front of the bus, may I add—now I have probable cause to hold them. And once that DNA comes back from the earring, I'm sure it will be a match to Jessi." He looked at Stephen. "Jessi told me that Todd was having an affair with Harriet. Those numbers in her diary were extensions at the college."

"That's where I'd seen them before. Tammy has a list of professors hanging on her wall to call when their books come in. The one is the dean's number." Cat hit the palm of her hand to her forehead. "I kept thinking about them, but then I'd think about Michael and get lost on a different trail. The numbers must have reminded me of my office number when I was a teaching assistant. I'd forgotten that was how everyone said them. The first three numbers were all the same, so they would drop them when telling someone their office line."

"There were two," Stephen said, looking confused and pained at the indiscretion. His voice lowered as he asked a question it didn't look like he wanted an answer to. "Two numbers. Was she having two affairs?"

"After we figured the shorthand, we called both numbers. One was Todd's office number, the other the number of the dean. According to the dean, Harriet kept in close contact with him as they were building this case against the retreat. He denied any affair. From the way he spoke about Harriet, I believe his statement."

"The dean is the one behind cutting the retreat's funding. Harriet was just his Trojan horse. And bonus, as long as he kept her in front of him, he looked sympathetic. I think I'm filing a complaint with the board tomorrow." Cat squeezed the bridge of her nose. "Or maybe Monday."

"You're saying Jessi found out about the affair and targeted Harriet?" Stephen tried to get the discussion back on track.

"Exactly, except Todd assumed no one, including Jessi, knew about the affair. He was wrong; his wife had figured it out. Jessi says she followed Harriet out of the party on Saturday night. She asked to talk to her in the barn, then Harriet attacks her with a shovel. Then she left saying the woman was crazy."

"So she was alive when Jessi left?" Cat asked.

"That's Jessi's story. She thinks that Todd must have seen them going in the barn and follows them. He sees Harriet attacking his wife, who'd just lost a baby a few months before, and he snaps. Jessi is a little obsessed about the knight in white armor description of his actions." Uncle Pete sighed and picked up his cake. "Of course, Todd's version has the facts a little different, saying Jessi must have been the one who killed Harriet. He was just a scapegoat. The problem is both of them say Harriet died right after the party broke up at eleven."

"But the coroner said time of death was around midnight. Don't tell me she was suffering all that time." Cat felt horrified at the possibility.

"I don't think so. Jessi puts Todd at their house about eleven thirty. She asked her husband to throw away the zombie outfit. I'm thinking she passed out then." Uncle Pete took a bite of his cake.

The room was quiet as the truth settled in. Stephen sank into a chair. "I can't believe Harriet was killed over some stupid affair. I mean, if I'd found out about Harriet and Todd, I would have at least tried marriage counseling."

Deek turned and looked at Stephen. "Dude, seriously? That's what you got out of the discussion?"

Stephen turned red and rubbed his hands. "Don't get me wrong. I feel bad about Harriet. I loved my wife. But I think Todd and Jessi need anger management training."

"At the minimum," Uncle Pete agreed. "Anyway, that's all I came to say. I wanted you to know what I found out since the pictures you sent and the earring put the spot light on those two. Motive is a little wonky, but the evidence is pretty clear they were in the barn. I think Covington's going to have to replace two professors this semester."

THE MOOD at dinner was subdued but light. After finding out who had killed Harriet, everyone seemed to have a weight off their shoulders. Especially Stephen. He sipped his margarita and then set it down and turned to Cat. "Can I ask you a question?"

"Of course." Cat turned her attention from the discussion between Deek and Seth regarding the best snowboarding runs in the area. She had a feeling Deek was coming back to Aspen Hills in a few months for at least a long weekend.

"I don't want to ruin the mood or anything, but something doesn't make sense about the murder." Stephen passed the chips to Pixie who had nudged his arm right when he'd gotten Cat's attention.

"What's troubling you?" Cat turned all her focus on Stephen. She'd had an unsettled feeling since Uncle Pete's visit as well. Not that she thought he didn't have the right person, but something... Maybe the same thing was bothering Stephen.

"It's the costume. Why would Jessi dress Harriet in her own costume? That would point the finger directly at her." Stephen sipped his drink again. "I can understand wanting to talk to the woman your husband is sleeping with. Maybe trying to reason with her. Maybe even killing her. But all changing clothes did was point the finger right at Jessi. Everyone at the party knew what costume she was wearing."

Cat blinked, taking in the information. Stephen was right. Jessi wouldn't have changed costumes, even being upset. She pulled out her phone. "That's what's been bothering me, too. I need to call my uncle."

Seth caught her arm as she stood to leave the table to make a call. "Everything okay?"

"Everything's fine. I just need to talk with Uncle Pete for a second."

Seth dropped his hand as he looked from Stephen to Cat. "Don't be long or I'll come looking."

"You've always got my back, don't you?" Cat asked.

Seth nodded. "Always."

Cat left the busy dining room and found a quiet hall near the bathrooms. When her uncle picked up, she told him about Stephen's questions. "I knew something felt off when you were talking to us. I don't think Jessi killed Harriet. I think Todd came back later that night and tried to frame his wife for the murder."

"That would work and we should be able to prove it as long as our city traffic cams are working. We'll probably need to follow his trail to find where he stashed the shovel and the witch costume, but I'm assuming it's the dumpster near the Student Union. It's dumped twice a week. I can't believe I didn't think of this angle. I need to go visit with one of my suspects before I finish these charging documents."

Cat pocketed her phone and made her way back to the dining

room. It was time to announce the Word King or Queen for the session.

~

THE NEXT MORNING, Deek picked up the Word King mug that Stephen had won the night before. Shauna had designed the cups last month and ordered several with King and Queen in different colors. They'd given Stephen a mug last night but told him he could choose a different color if he wanted that morning. "Dude, this is sick. I can't believe you won. Not with everything you had going on."

"It's all a matter of consistency." Stephen poured more syrup on his waffle. "Little bits here and there make the words add up. You'll figure it out. And, I kept forgetting to update my word count on the chart in the living room."

"Thanks, old wise one." Deek shook his head and turned to Cat. "Are you taking us up to Denver?"

"No, Seth's driving you." Cat looked out the window. The storm hadn't come in yet and if the weather forecast was right, he should be back in Aspen Hills before the snow started. "I wanted to have one last breakfast with you guys before you leave. It's been a fun retreat and I hope you all got what you wanted out of your stay."

"More than what I expected. I thought it would be some writing and a few classes. I thought it would be more on me to get things done, but it felt like we were all invested in each other's progress." Pixie smiled at the group. "I didn't feel like it was all on me."

"That's the feeling you need to find when you go home. I know the three of you will continue to support each other and you have a group, so I'm not worried about my California crew. It's the other two that need to find accountability partners." Cat looked at Dalton and Stephen.

"Don't look at me. I've got the writer group at the bookstore." Stephen turned to Dalton. "Are you coming to the meeting on Wednesday?"

"You make it sound like a twelve-step group," Dalton complained.

"Yeah, I'll be there. And I've decided that I'm going to tell my school advisor what I've been working on. They can't help me grow if they don't know where I want to go, right?"

"Exactly." Cat leaned back and sipped her coffee. Another retreat in the books and they'd helped solve a murder as well. Talk about multi-tasking.

After the guests left, Cat took the last tray of plates into the kitchen. "All cleared out. What else do you want me to do? I can strip the beds."

Shauna was boxing up cookies and other treats. "Actually, that's on Monday's list. Why don't you run this box of treats over to your uncle? That way we get the leftovers out of the house and I don't eat all of them."

"Are you sure? I got some words in early so I can help if you need me." Cat looked around the almost clean kitchen. Shauna had already started a load in the dishwasher and besides the tray Cat had just brought in, there wasn't much evidence that a retreat had even happened this last week.

"Please. With closing up this case, Pete called to say he wouldn't be at dinner tonight. So I thought he'd appreciate some sugar to keep him going." Shauna pushed the box into Cat's hands. "Besides, this way you get a walk in before the snow hits later this evening."

"Sound good to me." Cat set the box down and went to grab a coat from the hooks by the door. "Are you sure you don't want to come? You've been stuck in the house for the last week too."

"Actually, I'm thinking about taking Snow over to the arena later today. Especially since we're not doing family meal tonight. I've asked Seth to bring home a couple of those take and bake pizzas from that place we love in Denver." She glanced at her watch. "You better get going, I told your uncle you'd be there soon."

Cat put on her coat and then grabbed the box. "Okay, you're missing out. But I get it if you'd rather spend time with your horse than me for a bit."

Shauna laughed and Cat made her way outside. The chill was there, not freezing, but she could tell the seasons had decided to change. Winter had arrived and would be bringing presents like snow and ice soon to change the outside to a magical white wonderland. It was one of the things she loved about living in Colorado. They had all four seasons.

When she got to the station, a young woman she'd never met before sat at the reception desk. "Hi, I'm Cat Latimer and..."

"You must be looking for your uncle. I'm sorry, Chief Edwards was called into a meeting just a few minutes ago. I'm Dolly. I'm the temp." The woman came around the desk and held out her hands to take the box. "He said you were bringing him some treats. I'll put them on his desk. The man eats too much junk, but at least this won't be full of stuff like what he gets out of the vending machines. I bet his girlfriend is going to have a fit when she comes to visit."

Cat liked Dolly. She seemed to have a healthy attachment to Uncle Pete as her boss not like Penelope. "Make sure you grab a few of the cookies. Shauna has to be the best baker in Aspen Hills."

Dolly laughed. "I think my mom would argue that point, but I'll try the cookies and let you know. Have a great day. The storm is supposed to dump five inches tonight. Can you believe it?"

After she left the station, she decided to walk through the older section of town. She loved the big houses that, like hers, used to be part of the college. The past presidents and college deans were built houses to live in when the college was first founded. Now, over the years, the college had sold off the houses and they'd been remodeled and updated. But it still felt like she was walking in the past.

When she passed by Dante Cornelio's house, she could see from the black cars parked in front that her friend—or Michael's friend, really—was in residence. Uncle Pete and Seth didn't like her talking to Dante, mostly because of his status with the family that founded Covington. Being friends with a mob boss was problematic. But she liked his quick wit and he was the last tie to Michael that she had. Marrying Michael had been a mistake, but she had loved the man once. It was a part of her life she couldn't just forget.

As if she'd conjured him, Dante came up the street. He was dressed in a long wool coat and a wool hat. A red scarf was the only break in the black that covered him from head to toe. She'd never seen him wear color, especially not red. Dante was also the only man she'd never seen in jeans. She'd seen pictures of him and Michael when they were in college, and he'd worn jeans then. But in person, he was always dressed like he had an important business meeting in ten minutes.

"Dante, nice to see you." She stopped and looked up into that handsome face. Women fell for him fast, mostly because he looked like a dark god. But lately, Cat had seen worry and pain in the perfect face and blue eyes. The new responsibilities in his family business didn't seem to be settling well on him. "You look tired."

"You, on the other hand, look refreshed. And on a Sunday after your writing retreat finishes up. You must thrive on the energy." He squeezed her arms in a friendly half hug.

"Actually, the retreat drains all the life out of me. It's like a literary vampire that sucks my energy. Next week I'll sleep in late and try to not think about anything important." She blinked as she realized she was having a talk with Seth about their relationship tomorrow. Maybe that hadn't been the best planning. "So are you just out for a walk?"

"Actually, I just came from your house. I left the paperwork on the last of the estate distribution along with a check for you from Michael's share of the Denver building." He paused a minute. "You are no longer tied to the family business at all."

"Please tell me you gave most of it away. I don't want dirty money." Cat saw his wince at her word choice, but she didn't blame Dante for getting Michael into this problem. That had been his brother. A brother that had run the family but was now deceased. A role that Dante had taken after the death. "I'm sorry if that hurts, but I just can't."

"I know your feelings. The only source of the money in the check I left was for Michael's initial investment plus his share of the actual increase in valuation of the property. I hope you put it away and replace that roof next year. These old houses, they tend to have a lot of upkeep. I would hate to see Warm Springs Resort look less than perfect." Dante had replaced the wince with a smile. "Anyway, it's all there and Michael's estate is now closed. I'm sorry for your loss."

She put a gloved hand on his chest over his heart. "I'm sorry for your loss as well. I know you loved Michael as a brother."

Dante blinked back tears, which surprised Cat. "He was more than a brother."

Then he stepped around her and headed to his house. "Nice to see you, Catherine."

The moment was over. Cat wondered if she'd ever see Dante again. She'd made it clear months ago that she wasn't interested in a relationship. That she and Seth were serious this time. And yet, now that it was possible that they weren't, Dante had moved on.

Which was for the best.

When Cat got home, she noticed the flowers on the kitchen desk. Shauna was folding laundry. "Hey, the secret admirer strikes again?"

Shauna blushed and nodded to the table. "You have an envelope."

"Yeah, I saw Dante on my way back. He said he dropped it off." Cat pushed the envelope to the middle of the table, then poured herself a cup of coffee. "Michael's estate is finally settled. There's check in there. I'm going to put it in an account for the house. Just in case we need something."

"That seems logical." Shauna folded the last towel, then set the basket on the floor. "So how much is it?"

"I have no idea. Dante suggested putting it away for a roof. So probably a few thousand at least." Cat laid her head on the table. "I can't believe it's over. My life with Michael has been tied up in a bow and put into that envelope."

"Your life with Michael was over when the divorce went through," Shauna reminded her. "This is just the aftershocks. Like getting the house."

"Tomorrow, I'll see if I've still got a life with Seth." She didn't lift her head from the table. She didn't want to see Shauna's reaction.

"Cat, I live with the two of you. If anyone can make a relationship work in this crazy world, it's you guys. Just talk to him about how you're feeling. Just take a step." Shauna sipped her tea. "Relationships don't make sense until they do."

Cat lifted her head and saw the flowers. Flowers that someone in Shauna's life had brought her. Her eyes blinked. Wait, Shauna had gotten flowers at the same time as Dante had dropped off the paperwork? And she'd been insistent that Cat take the treats to Uncle Pete. Almost throwing her out the door when she'd checked her watch for the time.

She turned and looked at Shauna who had dropped her gaze. "No. You're not."

"I'm not what?" Shauna stood and picked up the laundry basket. "I need to put these away before the next load is dry."

"Your secret admirer is Dante?" When the words came out, it made sense. The red scarf on the black outfit. She'd never seen Dante with more than a grey scarf. But red matched Shauna's hair. He might be a little older, but so had been Kevin. Everything fit. "Oh my goodness. When did that happen?"

Shauna's face bloomed as red as her hair and she hurried to the door. "I don't know what you're talking about."

Cat sat in the kitchen for a long time after Shauna had left. She was happy for her friend. A little nervous because of who Dante was, but the match made sense. It wouldn't be an easy relationship, but Shauna was an adult. And, there was good in Dante, he just needed to figure out what he wanted. A life outside the family or one with someone who loved him for who he could be. Like the match between her and Seth.

Relationships never make sense until they do.

Cat went upstairs to her office to finish the book. She was close now. And there wasn't any angst around for her to worry about besides writing The End. Life at 700 Warm Springs Drive was good.

ST. LOUIS' BEST GOOEY BUTTER CAKE

Recipe

Hi Readers –

Shauna's a baker and that's my favorite part of cooking as well. Baking the cookies, the cakes, the pies, and even bread. But I'm more rustic than delicate in my food preparations. As I'm getting ready to move from the St. Louis area to Tennessee, I wanted to give you one more St. Louis tradition – Gooey Butter Cake. I've done this in chocolate for Christmas, but this vanilla version will be perfect for a summer cookout or a spring get together.

Lynn

Vanilla Gooey Butter Cake

Pre-heat oven to 350 degrees.

Mix together – Beat for one minute.

- 1 white cake mix
- ½ cup of melted butter
- Two eggs

Press mixture into a greased 13x9 pan.

In a clean bowl, beat cream cheese until fluffy

Then add –

- ½ tsp vanilla
- 2 eggs
- 3 cups of powdered sugar

Gently cover the top of the cake mix in the pan with this topping.
Bake for 40-45 minutes.

Cool and then sprinkle ½ cup of powdered sugar over the top before serving.

Looking for more Cat Latimer? You can buy the series in digital, audio, or print format at your favorite retailer.

THE CAT LATIMER MYSTERIES
A STORY TO KILL

Sign up for my newsletter at www.lynncahoon.com to stay in the loop on new releases and other fun stuff.

LEGAL BITS

Caught Dead to Write: A Cat Latimer Mystery by Lynn Cahoon

Published by Lynn Cahoon
  www.lynncahoon.com
  Copyright © 2022 Lynn Cahoon

Cover by Earthly Charms

Made in the USA
Columbia, SC
21 July 2022

63824716R00087